TREY

7 Brides for 7 Blackthornes, #7

CHRISTIE RIDGWAY

PRAISE FOR CHRISTIE RIDGWAY

"Emotional and powerful...everything a romance reader could hope for." --*Publishers Weekly* (starred review)

"Ridgway's feel-good read, with its perfectly integrated, extremely hot, and well-crafted love scenes, is contemporary romance at its best." --*Booklist* (starred review)

"This sexy page-turner [is] a stellar kick-off to Ridgway's latest humor-drenched series." --*Library Journal*

"Equally passionate and emotional, this tale will quicken pulses and firmly tug on the heartstrings of readers across the globe. An excellent story that you hope won't ever end!" --*RT Book Reviews* (Top Pick)

"Sexy, sassy, funny, and cool, this effervescent sizzler nicely launches Ridgway's new series and is a perfect pick-me-up for a summer's day." --*Library Journal*

"Ridgway's latest addition to the Cabin Fever series is heartwarming and gives us hope that second chances are always within reach...This small-town, sweet romance is perfect to remind one that love almost always endures the test of time." --*RT Book Reviews*

"Pure romance, delightfully warm and funny." --*NYT bestselling author* **Jennifer Crusie**

PRAISE FOR CHRISTIE RIDGWAY

"Ridgway delights yet again with this charming, witty tale of holiday romance. Not only are the characters sympathetic, intelligent and engaging, but the sexual tension between the main characters is played out with tremendous skill. The plot is well constructed, and the characters' emotional responses are satisfyingly believable, both in dialogue and in action." -- ***RT Book Reviews***

"Ridgway's latest addition to the Cabin Fever series is heart-warming and gives us hope that second chances are always within reach...This small-town, sweet romance is perfect to remind one that love almost always endures the test of time." --***RT Book Reviews***

"Christie Ridgway writes a sizzling combination of heat and heart." --***Barbara Freethy***, *#1 NYT bestselling author*

"Ridgway rocks romance!" --***Bella Andre***, *New York Times and USA Today Bestseller*

"Christie Ridgway writes with the perfect combination of humor and heart." --*NYT bestselling author* ***Susan Wiggs***

"Kick off your shoes and escape to endless summer. This is romance at its best." --*NYT bestselling author* ***Emily March***

ALSO BY CHRISTIE RIDGWAY

7-Stud Club

All In (#1)

No Limit (#2)

Ante Up (#3), *Coming soon!*

Almost

Almost Wonderful (#1)

Almost Always (#2)

Almost Everything (#3)

Almost Paradise (#4)

Rock Royalty Series

Light My Fire (#1)

Love Her Madly (#2)

Break on Through (#3)

Touch Me (#4)

Wishful Sinful (#5)

Wild Child (#6)

Who Do You Love (# 7)

Love Me Two Times (#8)

In Hot Water Duo

First Comes Love (#1)

Then Comes Marriage (#2)

ALSO BY CHRISTIE RIDGWAY

TREY

7 Brides for 7 Blackthornes, Book 7
© Copyright 2019 by Christie Ridgway
ISBN: 978-1-939286-50-5

Visit Christie's Website
http://christieridgway.net

CHAPTER ONE

TREY BLACKTHORNE SHOVED HIS HAND THROUGH HIS SHORT dark hair and made a mental note to schedule a trim. A quarter-inch past business-length and it turned unruly. Trey didn't like unruly—it didn't suit him and he didn't have time for it. As Graham Wallace Blackthorne III, hence "Trey," he had time for his role as Blackthorne Enterprise's Executive Vice President of Operations—the position just below his father's as CEO—and not much else.

"Hey." His oldest cousin Phillip walked up, the oldest of three who'd come to live with Trey's family when they'd been orphaned by an airplane crash. They'd been raised as siblings, all seven—Trey and his three brothers, Phillips and his two—together. The other man slid onto another of the leather chairs pulled up to a gleaming wooden table in the Vault, the whisky pub attached to the boutique distillery in King Harbor, Maine. The expansive space held an old, gleaming-with-wax wooden bar, an extensive display of call liquors, paneled wood walls, and parquet floors. Rich wool rugs decorated with bold patterns covered them, along with tables and leather-covered seating—armchairs, club chairs, ottomans, and couches. It was their family's pub, it poured their family whisky, and it was a common gathering place for their family members when they spent time at the family estate during summers and holidays.

Family was pretty much the only other thing Trey had time for besides his job at the company headquarters in Boston. "Hey, back," Trey said, taking a sip of the smoky concoction that was made with the same recipe their grandfather had brought over from Scotland. Though Blackthorne Enterprises had gone in other profitable directions over the years, whisky was at the heart of their success. If Trey didn't have his future sewn up in overseeing the totality of the family empire, he sometimes imagined spending his days at the original distillery that was adjacent to the pub. The scientific, methodical aspect of the process appealed to the part of him he expected came directly from his father—the part that eschewed emotion for order, numbers, and facts. The creative side of making the liquor appealed too, probably because it was so foreign to his nature.

"You're more quiet than usual," Phillip observed now, eyeing Trey over his own glass of amber-colored liquid. "Something bothering you?"

Instead of answering, he reached into the front pocket of his jeans and drew out a well-worn horn box designed to hold a pack of playing cards. He ran his thumb over the almost-translucent surface, a habit he'd picked up from his paternal grandfather who'd given Trey the box and the set of poker cards inside it before his death.

Those original cards were safely stored in his desk, but in their place was a high-quality set of cellulose acetate. It wouldn't survive the world's end, but anything close to it, yeah. Without speaking, he shuffled the deck and then began dealing the fifty-two pieces of plastic face down between him and his cousin.

"War," he finally said, picking up the top card on his pile.

Phillip sighed. "Don't you see that now I have Ashley I'm a lover and not a fighter?"

Trey had to grin. "You hate to lose just like every other Blackthorne. Chicken?"

As he knew it would, the comment caused his cousin to snatch up a card. They slapped them down on the center of the tabletop in unison, face up.

Chuckling, Trey said nothing as Phillip slid the king of spades—his—and the three of clubs—Trey's—toward his side.

Silent play continued until the dealt cards were exhausted and Phillip's win pile showed decidedly higher. The other man looked up, smug as only a younger family member could be. "I should have bet you something."

Trey eyed him, noting the strong Blackthorne features, the too-long-for-the-conference-table hair, and the grit of three-day-old beard on his jaw. "You should get a shave," he said, in a tone he recognized as his father's.

Instead of taking offense, Phillip only laughed. "You sound more like Uncle Graham every day."

Ignoring the jibe, Trey gathered the cards and began shuffling again. "Best two out of three?"

His cousin glanced at his watch. "Shouldn't you be on your way home to your fancy Boston condo? The lights go on at Blackthorne HQ early tomorrow morning and you've—what?—taken off a whole twenty-four hours?"

At the mention of work, a hovering headache he'd had for days, maybe weeks, maybe months, tightened its vice grip around Trey's temples. *Damn.* The thought of his weekday routine shouldn't give him grief like this. But he'd been unsettled the entire summer.

Two men heading toward their table drew his attention. Even in the dim light coming from the deer-antler chandeliers spread throughout the pub, he recognized their height and their athletic grace—a shared Blackthorne trait.

They moved with an unmistakable resolve and Trey had a sudden desire to take his cards and start running—but Blackthornes weren't cowards. So he merely blanked his expression as his brother Devlin, second of four, and his cousin Brock, last of three, drew out chairs and dropped into them, one on either side of Trey. They both had their own whiskies in hand and he swallowed a curse. If he'd noticed them pausing at the bar he'd have had time to slip out the back door.

It didn't take clairvoyance to know they wanted something from him. His head's pounding redoubled, yet still he didn't budge from his chair. They didn't call him the family fixer for nothing.

Laconic greetings exchanged, Devlin stretched out his long legs. "Nana got a parking ticket."

"Already taken care of," Trey said, almost smiling despite the pain at his temples. The eighty-six-year-old had a standing weekly appointment with her hairdresser, a woman nearly as old as she. The lady operated her beauty business out of her home on the outskirts of King Harbor's small, picturesque downtown, and Nana remembered a time when parking zones didn't exist there. She knew damn well what red-painted curbs indicated, but just chose to ignore it.

"Good," Dev said, then cleared his throat. "And, uh, one of the kids from my sailing program could use a meet with our state representative. There's a scholarship she's after and—"

"Send her info to my assistant. I'll put in a word and Jer will handle it."

Brock's hand came up. "I've got one," he said, and took a sip from his glass, his white teeth showing as he drew it down his throat.

Raising a brow, Trey looked to his cousin. The other man was Senior Vice President of Brand Management of Blackthorne Enterprises, so they worked on the same floor, often on the same projects, and shared the same commitment to the company and its many branches. He knew his cousin to be dedicated and driven, but the last few weeks had blunted some of Brock's sharper edges. Or, more correctly, it was a woman who'd done that. "What are you talking about?"

"I hear that Ross got a speeding citation last time he was in town."

"You mean the last time he blew through town, right?" Trey had to smile now, thinking of the third Blackthorne brother who had immersed himself in the building and racing of cars since an early age. "I don't think I can fix that one, as it might have been someone who looks and sounds a lot like me who tipped off Sergeant Lincoln as to where he might locate an officer with a radar gun."

Brock laughed, shaking head. "Really, Trey?"

"He drives too damn fast," he answered, not regretting his scheme for an instant. "Especially when he has concerns other than himself right now." A woman had caught his eye too, it seemed, and permanently.

"Speaking of concerns," Dev began, straightening in his seat.

Uh-oh, Trey thought, though he'd known it would come to this.

"We've got to do something," his brother continued.

Trey knew that "we" was going to turn into a "you" if he

didn't derail the conversation ASAP. "Speaking of romance, how's Hannah?"

Devlin's brows drew together. "You want to talk romance?"

Not particularly. Six of his seven closest relatives, his three brothers and all three of his cousins, had partnered up over the summer. He'd found it only served to underscore the distance he felt between himself and the Blackthornes of his generation. Before, he'd chalked it up to being the eldest, the one birth had bestowed with the heavy mantle of the family legacy. Now he thought temperament might play a part as well. Finding a soul mate seemed much too…whimsical for his prosaic nature.

Trey wouldn't recognize whimsy, let alone love, if it bit him on the ass.

Phillip set down the glass he drained with a clack. "All right, let's have it," he said, turning to Brock. "Has the Black-thorne Q-rating taken a hit over the summer?"

Trey stared at his cousin. He went his own way and spent most of his time raising money for a nonprofit benefiting kids who'd lost their parents. When had he learned to throw about marketing terms?

Brock looked as surprised. "You know about the measure-ment of a brand's appeal?"

Phillip frowned. "I have a brain."

Maybe they needed to work harder at getting him and his gray matter under the Blackthorne umbrella. "We should schedule a talk in my office," Trey told Phillip.

"Let's keep to the topic at hand," Dev said. "We need to talk about Mom. We need to do something about Mom."

There it was. Trey briefly closed his eyes, but that wouldn't stave off the conversation, because Brock wasn't going to let it go either.

"He's right, Trey. We've got to get a handle on this situation with Aunt Claire."

"This" had started in May, during a big bash thrown in celebration of Claire Blackthorne's sixtieth birthday. Instead of kicking off the summer season in style, his mother had interrupted the festivities and in front of friends and associates declared she was done with being unappreciated by her husband and always coming in second to the business. There'd been a mysterious reference about keeping some secret for her husband.

Finally, suitcases in hand, she'd stalked out of their King Harbor home. Though the company security team had tracked her right away to some friends' apartment in Paris, she'd refused to talk about the situation over the phone and only responded—cryptically—to texts from the seven Blackthornes she'd mothered. For his part, Graham had remained just as stubbornly in the States and still hadn't spoken with his wife.

No one knew what the hell was meant by a secret, but it had chilled Trey enough that he hadn't pressed his father too hard, who remained nearly mum on the issue. All he would say is he expected his wife to come to her senses shortly and return home.

"Clearly Dad's not going to start talking," Devlin said, leaning forward. "Do you have any new insights into whatever there is to this situation and this secret?"

"You know as much as I do," Trey muttered.

"What we know is that we can't smother rumors as fast as they come to life," Brock said. "And I realize that the photo of Dad with Sarah McKinney getting posted everywhere on social media didn't help."

The young woman in the suggestive shot was at the periphery of a big Blackthorne business deal and because the biographer his cousin was wild for had some involvement in its circulation, Brock had almost lost her. "Why don't you just focus on Jenna?" Trey advised.

"And who is going to focus on healing the fracture in the family?" Phillip demanded. "It's gotta be addressed, Trey. And we all know who's best suited for the job."

As much as he'd always willingly taken on the family fixer role, for some reason this problem felt too...thorny. Some inner voice, one he would have said a few months ago he didn't believe in—too *woo-woo* for his matter-of-fact disposition—cautioned him to stay well-clear. "Come on, guys," he said. "What am I supposed to do? Play marriage counselor?"

"Well, no," said Dev, the ghost of a smile turning up his lips, "considering the longest girlfriend you ever had lasted less than six months before she publicly proclaimed you cared more for your phone that you cared for her."

Relief coursed through Trey, even as he flinched at the description that sounded a lot like his mother complaining about his father. "Good, I'm glad we agree. Then—"

"But you're the one who should go to Paris and convince Mom to come home," Dev said. "Home where she can hash things out with Dad."

"Home where we can better control the messaging," Brock added. "There's never been a divorce in the Black-thorne family and—"

"Even I'm not so thick when it comes to women as to bring up the brand as an incentive," Trey said, frowning.

Phillip drummed his fingertips on the tabletop. "It's up to you how you manage it, Trey. Just find a way to bring her back and get to the bottom of that secret."

"The end of the fiscal year meeting is coming," he protested. But the three other men were looking at him, their gazes and their poses implacable, every inch of their Blackthorne Scotch stubbornness on display.

Hell.

"You better make it quick, then," Phillip advised, obviously reading his capitulation.

"You know we're more than prepared for the year-end meeting and your father or I will handle or delegate anything that comes up at the office," Brock said, pulling out his phone. "I'll even text Jer for you. Your assistant can book you on the first nonstop from Boston to Paris. You'll be there and back again so quick, there'll be no harm to you at all."

Trey swallowed a groan. *No harm to you at all.* Now why did that have the hollow sound of famous last words?

Mia Thomas lingered outside the door to her apartment building, the late September sun radiating off the sidewalk and the stone walls of the six-story structure shoe-horned between taller and more outwardly luxurious edifices. August temperatures, the month of her arrival in Paris, had broken records, and that heat seemed to be stored in the city's cement and masonry. But with the turn of the calendar the nights had lowered into the fifties and the combination made waiting on the sidewalk beneath the shade of a tree for her friend Claire Blackthorne's son to show no hardship.

No hardship? a soft inner voice inquired. *You're in* Paris! Mia smiled, and it caught the eye of a passing Parisian man who responded with an uplifted brow and a wicked grin. She couldn't help but laugh and call out "Bonjour," as he continued on his way, murmuring something too quick for her to catch.

Tossing her long chestnut hair behind her back, she

looked about herself again, fully expecting she'd recognize a fellow American upon his arrival. Though in her outfit of espadrilles, cropped linen pants, and vintage blouse—from Portugal, according to the flea market vendor who'd spoken slowly enough for her high school and college French to keep up—she thought Trey Blackthorne might be surprised to find that she also hailed from the United States.

He might be even more surprised by the information she'd agreed to impart.

She quelled a little uneasy flutter in her belly. Claire had assured Mia her eldest son was a reasonable man who would take the news well.

A mid-sized car pulled up the curb, a rideshare she guessed, and the back passenger door opened. A long leg poked out and the rest followed, a lanky figure in jeans and with a head of surfer-streaked dirty-blond hair. His blue T-shirt, advertising a brew pub in Redondo Beach, cinched his country of citizenship.

Could this be…? Her spine straightened, and another little flutter tickled her insides. The newcomer was undeniably attractive, even rumpled from travel and as he slung a large backpack over his shoulder. Maybe feeling her regard, he glanced over.

Unwilling to be caught staring, Mia shifted her gaze, but couldn't miss the feel of his own boldly, slowly crawling over her body, head to toe. Then back again, just as bold and slow.

Yuck. *Leeser*, a familiar voice said in her head, using the term she and her best friend Nicolette Arsenau had come up with at sixteen for leering losers…leesers.

The man moved on then, heading up the sidewalk and relief made her relax. Not Trey Blackthorne. What a disappointment it would have been to find he was Claire's son, despite his stepped-off-the-beach good looks.

Not that she was here for romance. Then that voice piped up again. *But—*

Far from it, she told the voice firmly. She had a mission to accomplish, despite how she might have avoided getting started on it. Why, she would have gone beyond the block today if not for the promise she'd made to Claire to welcome her son to the City of Light.

But that doesn't mean you can't also—

Mia firmly shut down the ghostly argument and people-watched to pass the time. The Parisians loved their dogs, all sorts, and she watched them prance and bounce and trot on the ends of their leashes. Maybe when she returned to Boston she'd get a pet to greet her when she came home each night, something to help alleviate the new loneliness that surely would descend with a vengeance when she finished her task here in France.

That's why a man in your life—

Desperate to shut down another inner conversation, Mia glanced about for distraction and found it in a woman strolling along the sidewalk. Dressed in classic black and white, her pants, blouse, and jacket ensemble fit her petite figure as if tailored for her—it probably was—and a lovely pair of heels extended her height. Claire Blackthorne dressed much more casually but with the same élan, and Mia's compliment on the older woman's style had been the icebreaker that led to a friendship that led to this moment now…Mia watching as yet another car pulled up to the curb. A taxi this time, and she drew nearer to the trunk of her tree as a traveler climbed from the rear seat to the sidewalk, a hardshell suitcase in hand. His other held a phone and his head was bent over it, hiding his face.

Unlike the previous traveler, this one she couldn't pin a nationality on with certainty. His charcoal suit—striped tie peeping from a side pocket—pale blue dress shirt opened at the throat, and steel watch strapped around his wrist weren't conclusive. Neither the short, barbered cut of his glossy dark hair. They shouted successful businessman in any language, however, a breed Mia knew well from her years teaching art at a private middle school that catered to children who didn't succeed in traditional educational environments. Turned out, though, that their parents often had highly traditional expectations for their progeny and not always appreciated or even accepted their childrens' differences.

Most of the men who came into her classroom dressed like this one were autocratic, impatient, and difficult to get along with. Was this person just another stranger arriving in the neighborhood, or…?

Claire should have shared a photo of her son, Mia thought. Then she'd be sure not to mistake him.

The man shoved his phone in his pants pocket and lifted his head.

Mia's heart stopped. His masculine features were all angles and straight lines, a face that would photograph best in black and white, light creating intriguing shadows that would catch the eye and keep it. He was approaching his midthirties, she supposed, and he could use his image to sell men's designer cologne or luxury watches or cars that cost more than decades' worth of her salary. Not clothes, though. While his tall body could be called lean, he had too much muscle mass for the gentleman catwalks.

She couldn't imagine him strolling down a fashion runway anyway. As he strode toward the apartment building, he moved with a purpose and an air of can-do—if not let's-do-it-*now*—that only a month away from the States Mia recognized as wholly American.

He pulled out his phone again, so as he passed her he

didn't appear to notice her presence half-hidden by the branches of the tree. But he was close enough that she smelled his soap…he was actually close enough to touch. Still, Mia waited until he approached the front door of the apartment building and he was staring at the names listed on the intercom system.

"Mr. Blackthorne?" she called.

He turned as she stepped away from the tree. His gaze fixed on her face and she twitched, her heart performing a half-skip in her chest.

He looks tired, she thought. Before, she'd noticed the outlines of him, what she'd first sketch with her charcoal on a page of her drawing pad. But at second glance, she saw the arc of fatigue beneath his lower lashes, the half-mast cast to his eyelids, and his full lips, turned down in a frown.

"Can I help you?" he asked, his voice raspy, again as if he was on the edge of exhaustion or had just awoken from sleep.

The sound of it skittered down her spine and she shoved her hands in the pockets of her pants instead of rubbing them against the new goose bumps rising on her upper arms. "I'm Mia Thomas," she said, moving forward. "And it's how I can help you."

His gaze didn't wander from her face.

Realizing her last words could be taken the wrong way—flirtatious or worse—she felt her cheeks heat. She withdrew keys for her pocket. "I mean I have keys to your mother's apartment. She asked me to greet you and let you in."

He blinked slowly, confirming her sense he was ready, in short order, to nod off.

"Let's get you settled inside," she said, bustling forward and opening the front door using one of the keys on the ring. "You can take a nap upstairs."

"I don't take naps," he said, in near the same tone a child

declared "I'm not cranky," and she hid her smile as she gestured him into the foyer. The marble floor gleamed and a large arrangement of fresh flowers sat centered on a round table.

Mia pushed the button to open the elevator and only stepped inside once he had. In the small space, he stood behind her. "'P' for penthouse." She touched that button next, and the car jerked, then lurched upward.

Mia's balance faltered and she took a quick step to regain it. At the same time, Trey Blackthorne's hand shot out, belying his fatigue, to grasp her shoulder. He pulled her back against his large frame to steady her.

Warm muscles, the hint of citrus and spice, a firm hold that made her own body want to melt. Swallowing, she side-stepped away, slipping from his hand, and braced against the elevator's inner wall. "Thank you," she said.

"It seems temperamental," he responded mildly. "Does it always act this way?"

"I have the basement apartment," she said, "so I only use the elevator when I visit your mother. And we usually meet at the café on the corner."

The elevator halted, this time the movement smooth. Mia stepped out of the car, glad for more oxygen to share. On this level a hall runner covered the marble floor and she followed it to the entrance leading into the apartment. Then she slid the key into the lock and pushed the door fully open, giving him the full effect of the beautiful space.

He stepped around her, and his gaze roamed the many windows with their fantastic views of the surrounding city. Though the building wasn't as tall as others, plenty of light poured through the glass and warmed the formal space with its gold-and-white carpets and pear-colored upholstery. On the walls not covered by windows hung an eclectic collection of frames, some holding oil paintings, some watercolor, some were shadow boxes displaying lovely objets d'art.

"This apartment, well, this entire building belongs to Mr. and Mrs. Caine," Mia said.

Trey nodded. "Sterling and Isabelle? I know them. She's president of the Friends of the Roger Belton Art Museum. My mother is one of the patrons."

"Yes." That's how Mia knew the older couple as well—through the museum. Housed in Boston, it displayed an extensive collection of Asian, European, and American art.

"They let Mom borrow their personal apartment," he said.

"Yes." Not wanting to get into the why of Claire's flight from Maine—not that Mia knew any details, actually—she gestured with her hand toward the hallway. "This way to the guest bedrooms."

Opening another door, she indicated the space. "There's an en suite attached."

He brushed past her to set his case on the luggage rack near the closet door. "Thank you…miss…" Clearly exhaustion had descended as he crossed to a wing chair and dropped heavily into it, then scrubbed his face with his hand. "I'm sorry, I've forgotten your name."

"Mia." She ventured closer, narrowing her eyes. "Are you coming down with something?"

He managed to look both affronted and about ready to keel over at the same time. "Of course not. I never get sick. And I have to return to Boston as soon as possible. Tomorrow, I hope."

She hid her wince, because if his hope included seeing Claire, it was certain to be dashed. "Mr. Blackthorne, frankly, you don't look well."

"It's Trey." He scrubbed his hand over his face again. "And I'm fine. I just need to talk to my mother and my world will get a whole hell of a lot brighter. When did you say I can expect her back?"

Mia shoved her hands in her pockets again. "I didn't say. I can't say, not exactly. However, she told me to ask you to wait."

He stared at Mia, a picture of privileged masculinity, the scion of the wealthy and powerful Blackthorne family, accustomed to getting what he wanted, when he wanted it. "What?" He cleared his throat. "Wait?" Clearly a foreign word to him.

"Yes, wait," she affirmed. "Indefinitely."

CHAPTER TWO

SQUINTING, TREY TRIED TURNING HIS POUNDING HEAD IN THE direction of a new sound. Someone was moving about his office. Though unlike him, he must have had one or two too many the night before when he'd been at the Vault. With…

He recalled Devlin and Brock, maybe another?

Light from an unknown source pierced the millimeter of space between his eyelids. He winced, and his hand crept up to cover them. "Jer," he said, naming his assistant. "Why are you here so early? Have I forgotten a meeting?" Groping around for his phone, he found only soft fabric instead of the hard surface of his desk. *What?* Nothing made sense.

A cool palm pressed his forehead.

At the sensation, his body jackknifed, and only then did he realize he'd been flat on his back but now sat upright. He forced his eyes open and the room spun once, twice before settling. The facts of his current situation came into clear focus as well.

Paris.

He'd fallen asleep on a couch.

It was morning now and the sun shone through that bank

of windows, its light a hundred recently sharpened knives. He closed his eyes again but not before taking in the feminine figure nearby, a silhouette against the painful brightness.

Mia.

That was her name.

She'd let him into the apartment the day before and then vanished like a genie after delivering the news that his mother wasn't in the city and expected him to wait upon her return.

Genie. Instead of gnashing his teeth over the position his mother had put him in, his thoughts slid back to that—genie.

No, his thoughts returned to *her*, Mia, who had struck him as something otherworldly at first glance. Maybe more of an urban mermaid, he decided, because of her rippling brown hair with its copper and gold highlights and her eyes that changed like brook water, from green to gold to a warm brown.

"Are you okay?" she asked, in a low, melodious voice. "Should I call a doctor?"

"Of course not," he said, bracing before opening his eyes again. Trying not to wince, he let the flooding sunlight assault him once more. "I never get sick."

She crossed by him to sit on the sofa. The movement didn't stir him, the cushions were so stiff they had no bounce, but the unsettling of the air as she passed made his eyebrows ache. "In any case," she said, "there's pain reliever tablets and a glass of water on the table in front of you. Shall I put them in your hands?"

That's when he realized his eyes had closed again. With effort, he forced his upper lids to lift and he carefully rolled his head to the side to look at her. The mermaid. Mia.

In different clothes than the first time—now sneakers, jeans, a white shirt that was plain except for the front buttons that might be actual seashells. Her heart-shaped face was framed by those cinnamon waves and he saw freckles now, a dash of more cinnamon across her nose and upper cheeks. Then she smiled, curving a pair of peach-colored lips. "Your hands?" she said.

He looked down at them, puzzled. Could she read even his muddled mind? Because sure, it might be really nice to frame her pretty face with them, holding her as he leaned down to—

"Do you want the water and the pain reliever?"

In your hands. It came back to him, what she'd said just moments ago. About helping him with the pain reliever. The idea of taking something for his discomfort appealed, but as he'd told her, he never got sick.

"I need more sleep," he declared. But first he had to check with the office. How long had it been since his last contact? "Do you mind finding my phone?" He disliked asking for help, but at the moment, rousing himself from the couch seemed impossible. "It's charging somewhere…"

The next time Trey woke, a mouthwatering smell filled the air. He breathed deep of it, his sense of time and place not yet kicking in. He opened his eyes, saw those windows but without the hurtful glare pouring through them. Across from where he lay on the couch, that young woman sat curled on a wide-cushioned chair.

His stirring seemed to catch her attention and she looked over. Smiled.

It pierced him as directly as the earlier sunbeams. Rattled by it, he looked down and noted he'd not changed since his plane flight and that he appeared as disheveled as he felt.

He hated not being at his best, especially in front of Miss Kind Smile. "Why are you here again?" he demanded.

She didn't take offense at his testy tone or his rusty voice.

"Your mother asked me to let you in yesterday afternoon and give you keys. Do you remember?"

"Of course I remember." Yesterday afternoon? That meant twenty-four hours had passed since he arrived.

"And I was here this morning. I have my own key and when you didn't answer the door, I was worried so I let myself in." She uncurled her legs and leaned her elbows on her knees, her pose earnest.

His gaze studied the way her hair curtained over her shoulders. The stuff looked thick and healthy, and the color of it changed, like her eyes, with light and shadow. Right now it was a rich brown, those spectacular gilded highlights hidden for the moment.

"You should eat," she said now. "I hoped to entice you with coffee and a croissant earlier, but you fell asleep again."

"Jet lag." Though he'd never suffered from it before. "I shouldn't be keeping you…"

"Mia."

He recalled her name, but it seemed more prudent to put a distance between them in this way because she'd seen him asleep and perhaps, just perhaps, slightly under the weather. It made him uneasy to think she'd witnessed him oblivious and vulnerable. It's why he didn't do sleepovers with female companions and made it a rule to end evenings in their beds so he could make his way to his own home before dawn.

"I'm sure Mom didn't want you to go to such trouble on my behalf, Mia," he said now, then hesitated. "Taking time away from your husband and perhaps, uh, children."

She grinned and held up the bare left hand that he'd already noted. "No man," she said, wiggling her fingers. "No kids either, except for my students."

That was conversational bait he refused to swallow. They were strangers, connected by the thinnest of threads, and he intended to keep it that way, because he was heading back to Boston in a matter of hours—he hoped. His parents' marriage had cracked, and his intention to get a handle on what was going on with his mother and the "secret" she'd alluded to didn't include getting sidetracked by a random neighbor, no matter how friendly and appealing.

Fine. She was gorgeous and under other circumstances, such as when he didn't hold the weight of this current chaos on his shoulders, he'd be pulling charm from his back pocket and doing what he could to get to know her better. Though he usually moved more slowly, surely coming from the same DNA as his youngest brother, the female-pleasing Logan, Trey could beguile a beautiful woman to spend time with him without a lot of preliminary buildup.

But not today. Not with that uneasiness that had been swirling about the family—and, frankly, inside of him—since Mom had hinted at some shameful past mystery.

"You should go," Trey said. It would be best for them both. She wouldn't have to waste her time any longer and he wouldn't have to pretend he didn't want to fall over for another lengthy nap.

She gave him a dubious eye. "You still don't look well."

"I'm great. Perfect. Fine," he countered, going for hearty. His energy continued to flag and he wanted her gone from the apartment before she got another glimpse of his weakness. Yeah, his ego was that big.

"How about the homemade chicken soup I brought?"

He stilled. That scent in the apartment. *Homemade chicken soup.* His ego couldn't hold out against his sudden hunger. "You made soup?"

"Madame Bonville who lives a floor above me made soup. I begged a bowl or two for you."

Trey frowned. "Should I pay—"

"Of course not!" Mia grinned. "She was happy to share after I described you in such piteous terms. Don't be surprised when she's shocked to find you not quite the frail and limp specimen that I described."

Only one word stuck to Trey's brain. "Limp?"

The woman's face flushed to pink. "Oh...um..."

Speaking of pity, he took some on her. "Maybe I should have that soup now." He made to rise to his feet, but she quickly jumped to hers.

"No, no," she said. "Let me bring it to you."

Trey couldn't calculate how long it had been since he'd visited the facilities and he couldn't face this woman another few minutes without a shower and a change of clothes. "I think I need to make the acquaintance of hot water before I meet up with that hot soup."

"Of course, of course." She gestured in the direction of a hallway. "You remember your things are that way?"

He'd find them, he thought, grimly getting to his feet and forcing them forward, along with his aching muscles and throbbing head. "I shouldn't be long." Then he glanced over his shoulder. "Or you can leave, of course."

Her next grin was as bright and enticing as the rest of her. "Not when I promised to tell Madame your reaction to her recipe using my best superlatives. It gives me a chance to practice my French."

Humanity returned with the application of soap, razor, comb, and toothpaste. Trey lingered in the steamy bathroom because though he felt more human he didn't feel completely revitalized. Upon facing Mia again, he wanted to present himself as cool, controlled, take-charge Graham Wallace Blackthorne III, a man not laid low by mysterious family upheaval or a pesky transcontinental virus.

Not that he actually was sick.

After running his hand over his smooth jawline, he judged himself steady enough to face her again. He tucked the towel around his hips and thought about the contents of his suitcase. Everything would be a wrinkled mess, but knowing his housekeeper who'd done the packing, he'd brought jeans and running shoes. A creased but clean button-down would have to do.

With his hand on the knob, he pushed open the door to the bedroom.

Holding his phone, Mia stood at the entry on the other side of the bed, framed by the white-painted threshold leading into the hall. Her eyes rounded and she froze, though her gaze dropped, taking in every almost-naked inch of him. "I, uh…" she gave a little wave of the cell, as her face flashed pink again, "…was just going to leave this in here for you."

Damn, his mother needed to get this place to stock better towels. They'd seemed perfectly adequate a moment ago, but now… His hand went to the knot he'd tied. *Don't fail me now.*

He reminded himself he was a cool, controlled, take-charge kind of man. So he told the area south of that knot to mind how Mia had described him to the soup-maker. Limp. *Stay limp.*

———

Mia answered the knock on her door the next morning, surprised to find a pale but otherwise alert-looking Trey Blackthorne, an empty, size large soup bowl in hand. Her gaze shifted to it, grateful to have something to focus on besides his face. Her initial quick glance told her that he was fully dressed, in jeans and a simple shirt that fit him like bespoke, its cuffs rolled to reveal dark hair-dusted forearms.

The man even had sexy forearms, she thought, which should be unsurprising after she'd seen his wide shoulder and muscled torso, covered in nothing but scattered water drops from the shower.

She hadn't handled that well, seeing him half-naked, and had stammered something about leaving the soup on the counter, tossed him his phone, then made quick tracks for the apartment exit. Ever since, she'd been berating herself for her gauche response to an almost-nude man in a towel. *But such a man*, that voice said in her head, teasing.

Mia ignored it. "Hello." Her attention remained on the soup bowl.

It was thrust in her direction. "Good morning. Thank you very much for the soup."

She grasped the ceramic. "You didn't need to—"

"Blackthornes always repay a debt."

Okay. The visit was obligatory. "All right. You're welcome, then." She cleared her throat and prepared to swing the door shut upon his leave-taking. "Have a nice day."

He stayed the action with a question. "May I come in?"

What could she do but invite him inside? "Um, sure."

Five strides over the threshold and he stood in the center of her small space, taking in the living area—dull-colored couch brightened with colorful throws and an adjacent small cushioned chair along with a "kitchen" that was no more than microwave, sink, tiny refrigerator, and a square of butcher block counter space. One half-opened door gave a glimpse of another room big enough for hardly more than a double bed. A second opening off the main area led to a tiny bathroom.

Meager light came in through grated windows at the street level, but through them she could see the bright blossoms of a red geranium overflowing a planter on the sidewalk. And, after all, this was Paris.

So why have you barely explored beyond the café on the corner?

"It's not the penthouse," Mia said to her guest. "It was likely originally designed for storage before being turned into a small furnished apartment. But the Caines were kind enough to allow me to stay here free for a few weeks."

"You know them?"

She nodded. "Through the museum."

"Oh?" He raised a dark brow that made her want to admit to every flaw and weakness.

Instead, she gestured toward the couch. "Would you care to sit? I can make coffee."

He glanced at the kitchen area. "Really? I couldn't figure out the contraption upstairs."

She recalled there was a fancy expresso—the word Parisians used—machine on the counter and a French press in a cupboard. "I could show you how to make a simple cup," she offered, before thinking better of it. Without waiting for his reply, she turned her back to prepare the beverage she'd promised. She had a French press too, and it was a matter of minutes before the fragrant scent of freshly ground beans laced the air.

He said he'd take it black, and she brought him a full mug, then picked up her own and perched on the edge of the chair across from his spot on the couch.

"I should thank you again," he said, glancing at her over the rim.

"Not a problem. You look almost fully recovered."

"I wasn't sick."

"Good to know." She managed not to roll her eyes. "Anyone might be tired out by the long flight."

"Yes. Sleep and that shower was all I needed."

Shower. At the mention, she felt her cheeks burn again. *Gah.* She looked away.

"I didn't know you were there," he said. "If I had, I would have come out of the bathroom in more than a towel or at least given you some warning. Sorry about that."

"Not your fault," she said quickly. "I intended only to leave your phone where you'd find it." How embarrassing, that he felt it necessary to apologize, when he'd been covered by more than half the Frenchmen she'd seen sunbathing along the Seine on her circuitous taxi ride from the airport to the apartment four weeks ago.

"Okay." He took another swallow of coffee, his dark eyes on her face.

"I've actually looked upon dozens of males in less, you know," she heard herself confess, and it only got worse from there. "Plenty, plenty of them naked. Lots and lots and lots of nude guys."

She fell back against the chair's cushion, her coffee almost sloshing over the top of her mug. "Oh, God. That sounds completely wrong, doesn't it?"

His lips twitched. "Perhaps an exaggeration? Lots and lots and lots does sound quite…experienced of you."

He was laughing at her, and while part of her felt a second small burst of mortification, another part of her liked the warm light in his eyes and the quick upturn of his lips. "While 'lots and lots and lots' may not be a precise mathematical term," she told him, keeping her expression serious, "it's actually not far off."

Hah! Let the too-attractive man chew on that.

"Oh?" Those thick brows rose, and he looked gratifyingly perplexed.

"Yes. Being around unclothed bodies is part of my training," she said, fighting her own smile as she wondered what conclusion he might make of that.

"Hmm," his eyes narrowed, his gaze turned assessing. "Quite the mystery. Give me a second to think on it."

She sipped at her coffee, enjoying the little game.

"An expert in—no, a regular spectator of—the opposite sex in an unclothed state," he mused aloud, then leaned forward to set his mug on the small-trunk-turned-coffee-table before him.

Mia saw the moment he noticed the thick, cardboard-covered sketchbook she'd left there earlier, its edges softened from handling. "You know the Caines through the museum. You're here in Paris." His gaze lifted to pin hers. "An artist? Yes, you must be an artist."

She made a face, disappointed. "You caught on too quickly. But yes, I have a degree in art and have spent a lot of time drawing nude models of all shapes and sizes, including men."

He grinned, relaxing against the sofa back. "I love being right," he said, tone smug.

There was that arrogant attitude she expected in a Black-thorne, particularly from the oldest son. It brought to mind Reed Stephens, the man she'd been seeing exclusively three years ago, who'd broken half the dates they'd made because he had important meetings or important clients who demanded so much of his important time. Her understanding had gone on much too long, according to her best friend Nicolette, who posited it made Reed feel just that much more powerful to last-minute cancel on his girlfriend whenever he wanted to boost his ego.

Finally, Mia had broken it off to Reed's great surprise and his emphatic statement that she'd "never get anyone better than him."

If he wasn't a leeser, he was most certainly a loser.

"Why are you frowning?" Trey asked.

She ignored his question just like she—mostly—ignored the voice that continued to pipe up randomly since her arrival in France. "I should clarify," she said, "that I'm not actually pursuing art as a career."

He glanced at the sketchbook. "No?"

"I teach the subject at a private middle school in Boston," she said. "That pays the bills. But I draw for my own amusement. And relaxation."

"Can I see—?" he asked, reaching for the thick set of pages.

"*No.*" She made a grab and secured the book against her chest. "That…it's… you know, personal." Clearing her throat, she tried sounding more casual. "I'm sure you understand."

It saved her from explaining why she'd already made several charcoal studies of him—his face, his chest, just his dark eyes, ready to ferret out things she wanted to hold private.

"Okay." He shrugged. "I don't know much about the artistic bend of mind." Standing, he withdrew a small box from his pocket, about the size of a deck of cards. But he didn't do anything with it except hold it in his palm and stroke it slowly with the edge of his thumb, an absent gesture.

Then, as if the caffeine had kicked in and turned him restless, he returned the box to his pocket and began prowling the space, peering out the narrow windows, running his finger along the spines of the paperback thrillers left in a narrow bookcase by some former German-reading resident, then stooping to examine the small hand-blown vase she'd found abandoned in a cupboard. It held a single peach rose bought at the local market, now blossomed to the point the flower resembled the puffy skirt of a prom gown.

Straightening, he glanced over at her.

"What?" She rubbed at her face. After drawing, sometimes she ended up with charcoal smudges on her nose, chin, or forehead.

"Your skin," he said. "It's like the petals of that rose."

"Oh. Uh…" *Thank you. The proper response is thank you.* "Thanks." A warmth kindled in her belly and she felt as flustered as a silly high school freshman being noticed by the handsome and charismatic senior boy.

With a little grunt, he made another lap of her living space, this time taking a longer perusal out her windows. With his back to her, he spoke again. "Do you happen to know what's going on with my mother?"

"Um…" Mia hadn't sworn a blood oath, but she wasn't sure about sharing any part of the conversations she'd had with the friendly, but sometimes sad and sometimes pensive, older woman. "We only met a few weeks ago. The Caines recommended I knock on her door and introduce myself upon arrival, since we both have ties to the museum—I regularly take my students there for lessons and inspiration."

"Mom wouldn't trust the keys to her apartment to just anyone. I assume you've talked and spent time together."

"We both enjoy the café at the end of the block," she admitted.

He turned to face her, his expression unreadable now. "Well, in case she didn't tell you, my dad threw her a big sixtieth birthday party last May at our place in King Harbor, Maine."

It wasn't a "place," it was a seaside estate, everybody knew that. The Blackthornes made their first fortune in whisky generations ago but now had other successful ventures. Race cars, she thought. And hand-built luxury boats. Hardly a holiday could go by without local news covering some spectacular party thrown at the King Harbor mansion and grounds, every inch suitably decorated to welcome and wow celebrities, statesmen, and ultra-successful business people.

"I'm sure the event was lovely," Mia murmured.

"It was a disaster," he countered flatly. "If you live in New England, I'm surprised you haven't heard about it. Gossip flies fast."

"I'm not aware." Because in the last eight months, she hadn't been exposed to her usual amount of media. Nothing much had pierced the heavy veil that had dropped over her last January, the heavy veil she'd yet to push off.

You're going to do that in Paris. Starting now.

"What exactly happened?" Mia asked Trey.

"That's just it, we don't know." He forked a hand though his short hair, which did nothing to disorder the locks. "Mom made a scene, accused Dad of caring about the business more than anything, including her and their marriage of thirty-seven years, then the next thing we know she's storming off with her suitcases, with the word 'secret' echoing in every-one's ears."

"What secret?"

"I suppose that means she didn't share with you, either." Trey started moving about again, his agitation obvious. "Dad put our security team to work and they traced her to Paris right away, but she refuses to take calls or say much in texts to me and my brothers and cousins. My father refuses to get on a plane and get to the bottom of what is going on with them and he claims ignorance of this alleged mystery."

"Maybe he just doesn't want to say what it is," Mia ventured.

Trey threw her a look. "There is no secret," he said.

But his vehemence made Mia wonder if he actually

believed that. "Your mom only told me she's here to pursue her interest in drawing and painting. She's found a group and a teacher. They're taking short trips about Europe as part of their study."

"No one's ever heard of this interest," he muttered. "Painting? She's known for her good taste in decorating and planning successful fund-raisers, but the only times I saw her draw anything it was with crayons or sidewalk chalk."

The image made Mia smile. When Claire talked of her four sons, and the three nephews that she and her husband had raised after their parents died in a plane crash, her devotion to them was palpable. She would have been the kind of parent that Mia had wished for her entire life—highly involved and willing to play. "I bet she made incredible Halloween costumes and threw fabulous birthday parties when you were young."

Trey stopped pacing, the expression on his face considering. "She did. Not one costume came from a store and our birthdays were not of the famous magician guest star or even the pony-rides variety. No five-star chefs, either. Once, she buried plastic dinosaur eggs and bones and we had an archeological dig. Another time we were all pirates for a day and she created a treasure map that she cut into pieces. We had to put it together and then work as a team to discover the buried treasure."

"Maybe she misses those opportunities to be creative," Mia offered.

"Maybe." Trey frowned. "It doesn't explain why she has to throw out the threat of some secret." On the move again, he headed for the bookcase once more. Instead of looking at the books, his attention focused on the promise-blue box she'd placed atop it.

Mia's heart jumped to her throat. The 6 x 6 square item

was something she'd crafted herself, years ago, from paper pulp and a mold and deckle she'd made with two old photo frames. She'd found them, the wedding portraits inside each slashed to tatters, abandoned in her mother's garage along with other detritus of her parents' unhappy union and nasty divorce.

"This is pretty," Trey said, and his hand moved as if about to pick it up.

Mia jumped to her feet. "We need to go."

He looked over. "What?"

"You need to take me out of here." She needed to get him out, too, before he asked a question she'd find herself powerless against answering. Escape from the apartment seemed the most expedient method.

"Why?" he asked, his eyes narrowing.

"Blackthornes repay their debts, right?" She ignored her own instincts that said it was unwise to continue their acquaintance and grabbed his hand on her way toward the door. "I'm hungry. Let's head out for a meal."

CHAPTER THREE

TREY'S HAND AUTOMATICALLY FLEXED AROUND MIA'S GRASP, not too hard, but enough to hold firm as they walked through her door and up the dim, narrow steps to the main apartment exit.

As they stepped onto the sidewalk into the midday sunshine, the warmth of it felt like summer but trees had dropped leaves that sprinkled the sidewalk. They flurried on the updraft of their moving feet. She glanced up at him. "You must be hungry too."

He nodded. "I could eat." More words were not available to him, a hell of a shock, because he'd never been at a loss like this. But the truth was, his focus couldn't expand beyond the sensation of her slim hand in his, a light weight that still sent a distinct buzz through his blood.

"'I could eat,' you say?" Her smile teased, and he felt that, too, another visceral jolt to his system. "This is Paris, sir. You don't eat, you enjoy."

Apparently enjoyment was a mere half-block away, at a café on the corner with a dim interior and doors that opened to small tables and chairs spilling on the sidewalk. Patio heaters hovered above them, but on a day like this one, people didn't even need jackets to enjoy their meals outside.

When she paused, he pulled out the nearest chair. "Here?" he asked.

"Here." She slipped free of his hand and settled, smiling again as he took a seat. "Do you speak French? Read it?" she asked, indicating the menu.

He shook his head, and leaned back in his chair. "A word here and there, like anyone else. When I come to the company offices here, they assign me a full-time aide who shames my lack with his linguistic skills. I think English is his fourth language."

"Oh." Her face fell. "So I'm not introducing you to Paris cafés. I should have guessed."

"But you are." He realized it was true. "When I've visited before, a business dinner or two is arranged. I'm in and out as fast as possible."

"You don't like travel?"

"No, I..." While children, they'd spent vacations in a variety of locales, their mother planning trips which blended history, culture, and outdoor activities enough to keep restless boys entertained. Their father had joined them for a few days here and there, but business had never allowed the CEO to fully enjoy their excursions.

And Trey, as had always been expected of him, had walked through the doors of the Blackthorne Enterprises headquarters in Boston at twenty-four and in the ensuing ten years had never taken the time for real vacations or "travel" in the way Mia meant. There'd been no leisure.

The arrival of the server saved him from having to expand on his answer. At Mia's offer, he agreed to her ordering for him, and discovered he was starving once his plate of steak frites arrived. An omelet appeared in front of Mia and then followed long minutes when they both ate in an appreciative silence.

Hunger sated, an expresso in front of him, he sat back in his chair and let his gaze rest on his companion. With her lips curved, she had her eyes closed, clearly relishing the moment. His own tension, tension he'd held for—years?—seeped away as he studied her, her peach skin and the skeins of her amazing hair. Then he thought of what else he knew of her... not much.

"Your school's in session this time of year, right?" he asked idly. "What's your purpose for being here in Paris instead of the classroom?"

Her lashes lifted. The sun lightened her eyes to hazel green. A beat of silence passed and then she glanced around her, calling for the waiter. "We each need a crêpe," she said, as he handed over his credit card to the arriving server. The bill was handled in mere moments and she was already out of her chair as he slipped the plastic into his wallet.

"I don't think I have room for anything else," he told her, as she took off down the sidewalk.

Her step hitched. "A walk along the Seine first then," she said. "I've been wanting to do that since I arrived."

He lifted a brow. What had the woman been doing besides passing time at the corner café where they clearly knew her? But instead of pressing, he silently let her set the pace. It wasn't far to the wide, busy river that defined the city as much as its famous landmarks. The pavement above the bank was busy with Parisians out for a stroll as well.

Again, he let his other concerns drift away as he watched the people. And their dogs. Lots and lots of dogs, and he amused himself by looking for similarities between them and their owners. A simple pastime, one he remembered from simpler days.

He realized he was smiling, and glanced at Mia to see that she was as well. Their gazes met.

"Crêpes," she declared, and turned back in the direction of their building.

They knew her at this little hole-in-the wall too, and he wasn't surprised once he realized how close it was to the apartment building. But they lingered on the sidewalk outside it to enjoy their treats and damn, he felt like a kid again, with sweetness in his mouth and warmth on his shoulders.

He chewed the last bite of the crêpe and threw the wrapper in a nearby trash can. "I decided to open a T-shirt shop in the town of Hanalei on Kauai," he said.

Her gaze swung to him. "What?"

"I was nine. I decided school was overrated, but not Hawaii and I was decent at making change. So I'd sell T-shirts at a store called Blackthorne's on the Beach in the mornings and hit the surf every afternoon."

"You didn't just think…hey, beach bum, and not worry about how to make a buck?"

He laughed. "I'm a Blackthorne. I was envisioning a business as much as a lifestyle."

"So…what happened?"

"What do you mean?"

"You could be selling T-shirts right this minute…well, if it was morning in Hawaii."

"Can you see me in a straw hat and a shell necklace?" he scoffed. "Barefoot and shaggy-haired?"

"Give me a minute." Her eyes narrowed as she looked him over. "Yes."

Trey blinked. "That's a first. Most people think I'm born-and-bred for the boardroom."

She shrugged and half-turned away. "Maybe because I saw you in just a towel and nothing else."

He stilled, struck by…something. "Hey…" he said, and with a hand on her shoulder, turned her toward him again. They were standing close enough to the apartment building that he could feel a warmth emanating from the stone exterior. It was nothing to what he felt under his hand, though, her flesh beneath her clothes heating at his touch.

"Hey," he said, again, his voice softer. He liked that his touch affected her, just as he liked her hair, her eyes, and the way she seemed to see him differently than everyone else.

One glimpse of him in a towel and now she could imagine him out from behind his desk. In a straw hat, for God's sake. The idea of it made him want to laugh.

And that made him feel…not nine, but nineteen maybe, or older, but certainly before he had a corner office and he realized his future looked just like his father's present. His hand moved from her shoulder to cup her cheek. Maybe this sudden sense of well-being, of being seen, or found or whatever you'd call it, was the legendary magic of Paris.

And then she confirmed it by boosting onto tiptoe and kissing him.

Warm lips, sweet taste. His other hand reached for her waist and he drew her closer, deepening the kiss by sweeping her mouth with his tongue. She didn't object, but instead edged closer, her breasts brushing his chest. His brief concern about their very public venue was shoved aside when her hand slid into his hair at the back of his head and he sank into the kiss until he was out of air.

His head lifted an inch and he looked into her eyes, deciding he was charmed by the impromptu meeting of lips. Enchanted, even. "Why'd you do that?" he asked.

Her smile only dazzled him more. "Didn't you want to? Everybody should share a kiss in Paris. Now we can both mark it off our bucket lists."

He didn't want to mark off anything. He just wanted more. "You owe me," he said, smiling back. Two could play the teasing game. "For subjecting me to, uh, such public exposure."

"Hmm." Another smile. "Your price?"

His forehead touched hers. "How about your secrets?" he asked, because now he was only more curious as to her presence here. He was curious about everything that made up Mia Thomas. "Ready to share?"

She took a breath. "Trey—"

"I can't believe my eyes," a new voice said. A familiar voice. Claire Blackthorne's voice, his mother. "You're in Paris, honey, without a tie and without your phone glued to your hand. Not to mention with your arms around a beautiful woman."

Mia, flushed and flustered to be caught kissing her friend's son on the sidewalk, had found herself following Trey's lead and taking on the older woman's burdens. After a quick embrace, Trey had Claire's suitcase and toiletries bag in hand while Mia now carried the expansive tote used for drawing and painting supplies.

"You two spoil me," Claire declared as she let them into her apartment. "I'm not elderly, you know, I can manage my own things."

She didn't look elderly in the least, Mia acknowledged. Like her son, she had an unforgettable face, with amazing bone structure that sixty years didn't diminish. Her silver-streaked dark hair was pulled back and coiled in a knot held in place by a silver comb. She wore a knee-length black tunic, its neckline embellished with an elegant design in metallic thread, over paisley black-and-white fitted pants and a pair of black ballet flats. Her right wrist was wrapped in several distinctive bracelets and on the ring finger of her left hand was a platinum wedding band and an engagement ring with an impressive diamond solitaire.

Mia noted Trey's gaze had landed on it, and she supposed him relieved that his mother hadn't divested herself of that symbol of her marriage. "Mom," he said now, setting down the items he'd carted in, "we need to talk."

Eager to give them privacy, Mia placed the artist's portfolio on the small table beside the front door. "I should leave you two to catch up."

Which would leave her alone to process that impulsive kiss she'd laid on the man. Her lips continued to tingle and her insides still felt weightless. What had she been thinking?

"Nonsense, Mia," Claire said, "there's no reason for you to go." She disappeared into the kitchen and at the sound of running water it was a good guess she was filling the teakettle. "I can predict everything my son is going to tell me."

Trey's expression turned stony as his mother's words floated from the other room. "Let's see. The Blackthorne Enterprises acquisition of the McKinney brothers' company is on track. This year's corn harvest also means good things for the whisky side of the business. Surely an order or two has come in to keep the boatworks busy. A new investment opportunity waits on the table and your father has taken it upon himself to be the sole investigator and judge of its potential. You boys—"

"Have had a very busy summer, Mom. Each of the other six has found a love interest and in every case it looks to be permanent."

A silence filled the apartment, then Claire emerged into the living area again, her expression signaling regret. "I know. They've shared via text. I've told them how pleased I am for their happiness."

Mia's heart ached for the other woman. She moved forward, not sure what to do, but willing to offer support and comfort—as Claire had provided her more than once.

But the other woman seemed to gather herself and her tone turned brisk. "So maybe it's well and good I left the country. Perhaps everyone in the family needed a little shake-up."

"Mom…" Trey sounded tired again. He crossed to a chair, dropped into it, and scrubbed his face with his hands. "These last few months have been more than a little shake-up."

Claire's face softened and she walked to her oldest son to put her hand on his shoulder. "You look worn-out. Have you been taking care of yourself? Getting out of your desk chair at least once every eighteen hours?"

"He was sick when he arrived here," Mia put in without remorse.

Trey glared at her. "I'm never ill."

"Of course," his mother said, patting him. "Blackthornes defy all germs and viruses."

"Exactly."

Claire glanced over her shoulder at Mia to share a look. They both shrugged.

"Enough about me," Trey said, taking his mother's hand in his. "What have you been doing all this time? Let me amend that. What the *hell* have you been doing?"

Her mouth pursed and her eyebrows drew together. "You sound more like your father every day."

He sighed. "Mom, you walked out without a word of where you were going."

"And I was found."

"As I'm sure you expected would happen. But we don't

know anything about this…this art teacher or this art group you've joined."

The whistle of the teakettle had her bustling away. "I don't have much time. I'm only here for a few hours to repack for our next field trip."

Trey closed his eyes and pinched the bridge of his nose. "Mom," he called out. "I can't go home without more information. You left after dropping a big bombshell with that talk of a secret."

Claire came back into the living area, a napkin in one hand and dismay written all over her. "I…I shouldn't have done that. I was upset."

"We got that, Mom. But don't you think you now owe us some kind of explanation?"

"You," she murmured, tears glinting in her eyes.

"*Me?*" Trey rose to his feet, his expression confused. "What are you talking about now, Mom? What about me?"

Biting her lip, Claire Blackthorne stood silent for a moment. "I'm not ready to do this," she finally said, balling the fabric she held. "I must pack. We're traveling to Provence today and I have to meet my group at the train station."

"I'll go with you," Trey said quickly. "We can talk on the trip."

"No!" Claire brought the napkin to her eyes for a brief moment before she dropped her hand. "I need a few more days. Please. Now that you're here, I…I'll gather my thoughts. I'll find a way to explain. Then we'll have a conversation."

He lifted his arms to his sides, clearly frustrated. "What am I supposed to do until then?"

Claire's gaze shifted to Mia.

Uh-oh, she thought, and began backpedaling toward the exit.

"You two can take the time to explore Paris," Claire suggested. At the idea, her whole demeanor seemed to brighten, her mouth curving and all sign of tears dissipating. "Mia has been meaning to do some real sightseeing and you might be just the incentive she needs to make that happen."

Uh-oh, Mia thought again, reluctant to get involved in the mother-son discussion but also unwilling to get dragged into their problems. "Claire," she ventured. "I don't think Trey has sightseeing on his mind."

"Sweet girl," the older woman said, and her eyes were so kind that all Mia's protests died. "Leave this to me."

Her son was made of sterner stuff. "Look, Mom, I can't be away from the office like you're sug—"

"Trey, take it from the person who's known you from the day you were born. You're thirty-four years old and you need to unwind before you find you're sixty-five years old like your father and still chained to your desk at Blackthorne Enterprises. Go about the city with Mia and I promise I'll sit down with you when I get back."

He frowned. "What you're asking for—"

"Is only three more days."

"Mom—"

"Don't 'Mom' me. Three days. I'm not wrong about this and my proposal is a good one for you. The most relaxed and happy I've seen you in years was thirty minutes ago when you were locked in an embrace with my beautiful young friend over there." With a nod at Mia, she disappeared into the kitchen again.

Trey looked over. Mia tried not to blush. It was merely a kiss, wasn't it, despite the fact his mother had caught them at it? There was no need to feel guilty or ashamed.

There was no reason to want to kiss him all over again.

"It's Paris," she said, as much of an excuse for herself as it was for him.

"Why have you been putting off your sightseeing?" he asked, his eyes narrowing. "What exactly has brought you here?"

Way to cut to the heart of the matter.

"Oh, well." She looked away. "It's pretty personal."

"I've told you about the Blackthorne imbroglio. You just witnessed what I'm up against."

"Right." She nodded. "Doesn't that mean you have more important things on your mind?"

He crossed his arms over his chest. "Call me a multitasker."

"Men aren't multitaskers," she scoffed. "Everyone—"

"Mia." His voice softened and in a blink he was standing in front of her, his dark eyes boring into hers. "Stop trying to sidetrack the conversation. Talk to me about why you're here and what's going on."

The weird thing was, she wanted to. Just as much as she'd wanted to kiss him.

"Maybe I can help," he offered now.

He couldn't, not really, this was her assignment to complete.

But with him alongside it might be easier, Nic's voice whispered in her head.

"You won't want to help, once I tell you," Mia said, addressing Trey. Then she corrected herself. "*If* I tell you."

"Try me." He took her hand in a light but firm grip.

She stared down at their joined fingers. What was happening here? Kisses, confidences, one man's simple touch filling her with so much…comfort and…joy. Like a Christmas song, she thought, giddy with it.

"Mia."

She tried one last time to draw away but he held fast. "It's a sad story," she warned him.

He just continued to look at her, and her need to confess every failing rose with each passing moment. *I say I forgot my father's birthday but actually I intentionally send him a belated card every year. I tossed in the trash the family Christmas ornaments my mother boxed up for me after my parents' divorce.* And in case that was all too one-note, *last summer I got so frustrated with the faulty scanner at the grocery store's self checkout that I put the ice cream in my bag without paying.*

Trey squeezed her hand. "I'm here, Mia."

But the point of all this was that Nicolette wasn't here! *Tell him,* her friend's ghostly voice whispered in Mia's head. *Tell Trey.*

"I have my best friend's ashes." The words burst from her. She chanced a glance at him.

"Okay." He didn't blink. "Your best friend's actual ashes?"

"Yes. Nicolette. She…she died last January."

"I'm sorry to hear that."

Mia tried to pull away again, but he didn't allow it. "We've been best friends since forever. She was closer than a sister to me…at least I think that—I don't have an actual sister. I don't have any siblings."

"What happened to her?"

"It was a stroke. She'd not been sick, she'd not had any symptoms that she shared with anyone, anyway."

"My grandfather died of a stroke. They call it the silent killer."

Mia bent her head. Silent killer. But at the news of her best friend's passing, she'd screamed at the unfairness of it all. Nicolette Arsenau, wild and fun, centered and sweet, both

Mia's rock as well as her kite. "Nic's parents practically raised me too, and they asked me to take her ashes to the city she always talked about visiting. That we were supposed to visit together."

"Paris."

Nodding, Mia kept her gaze on her feet. Part two of the mission she'd keep to herself. "There's a list of places she wanted to go here."

He didn't ask why she'd been stalling doing that very thing, though his mother had alluded to the fact. "Well, we've got three days to get through as much of it as we can."

She looked up. "No, really. I couldn't ask you—"

"You're not asking. My mom set the terms of the deal. You heard her, and I've learned just how stubborn she can be. If I want the answers I'm seeking, then for the next seventy-two hours, Mia Thomas, I'm all yours."

CHAPTER FOUR

TREY AWOKE, THE CELL PHONE ON THE BEDSIDE TABLE TO HIS right ringing. He blinked, trying to orient himself. Soft light slanted through a half-open doorway. It provided enough illumination for him to make out the face of the small antique clock sitting beside his cell. The hands said six o'clock, and it had to be morning. As the device rang again, his gaze lifted to the room's walls, covered with framed paintings of all sizes and shapes.

Paris, he remembered. A guest room at the Caines' apartment. Next he recalled his mother's exit from the apartment yesterday afternoon, bound for another trip with her "class" of drawing students. Her promise to return. The bargain they'd struck.

Hell. What version of Trey Blackthorne had agreed to take time off for something as frivolous as sightseeing?

The phone demanded his attention so he scooped it up, the screen displaying his father's name and number. On the US East Coast it was midnight. Trey stared at the phone for a beat, amazed his father had made a concession for the time difference.

He accepted the call and put the phone to his ear. "Dad? Thanks for waiting until dawn." Though a glance toward the curtain-covered windows testified the sun had yet to rise.

"You didn't check in yesterday."

His dad's disgruntled tone didn't surprise Trey and also served to settle him into his own skin—a welcome effect, as he'd felt out of sorts upon landing in Paris. Ever since he'd crossed the threshold of Blackthorne Enterprises HQ, MBA in hand, he'd been in constant contact with his father, willfully immersing himself in every deal and every detail. For as long as he could remember, it was the future mapped out for him. While his brothers and cousins had been under pressure to find their places within the company, it was Trey who had grown up fully aware it would be him and him alone at the helm when his father retired.

He'd never questioned or complained about that responsibility.

"Is there something I should know?" he asked.

"There's something *I* should know," his father returned. "You've seen your mother? Tell me how she is."

"Well enough," Trey answered. "We had a brief chance to talk."

"What did she say?" Graham demanded. "What exactly?"

"Not very much," Trey admitted. For a second he considered lying and saying she was sick, a well-meaning untruth that would get his father on a plane and result in a greater good—but no. "She's taking some art lessons and her student group was off to Provence so she was in and then out again."

"Art lessons?"

Okay, so the notion was new to his dad too. "I tried telling her—"

"What did *she* tell *you*?" There was a palpable tension in Graham's voice.

"Not much beyond the art thing," he said, then grabbed the bull by the horns. "But I really think you should come to France yourself, Dad. Finally get things straight between you two."

"Go into the Paris office today," the older man said, ignoring the suggestion.

Trey sighed. "Dad—"

"Let them see your face."

"Dad, really—"

"It's good for a Blackthorne to check in regularly."

Resigned, Trey sighed again as he pushed back the covers. "Is there anything in particular that you think needs my attention?"

"Meet with Guillaume and determine if he's having any trouble with those new import regulations."

"Guillaume is perfectly capable of handling his job, Dad," he said, even while knowing it wouldn't be enough to satisfy his father. "We don't need to micromanage."

A longstanding argument that never swayed Graham.

But before the older man could prove that once again, a different voice got on the line. "Hey, Trey."

Brock must have swiped Dad's phone from his hand. He was the youngest of the Blackthorne cousins, and he'd taken particularly to his aunt Claire, being only nine when he'd lost his own mother.

"Everything okay, cuz?" Trey asked the other man. "What are you and Dad doing at midnight?"

"We had a business dinner with the McKinney team that ran very late. Just thought you'd like to know it went well and the debacle over the photo is a dead issue," his cousin said. "We're back on track and full speed ahead—I expect the takeover from here will be seamless."

"Right." As Senior Vice President of Brand Management,

Brock saw any change through the lens of how it affected the promise the name "Blackthorne" made to the customer. His youngest cousin placed an extremely high value on the business...and on the family. Trey didn't fault him for either, of course. "You'll want to hear about Mom."

A hesitation betrayed just how much. "She seems okay?" Brock asked.

"Stubborn. Full of energy. Clearly sad about missing out when we talked about how the six of you have gotten serious about romance."

"Did you remind her of her own romance and marriage?" Brock asked. "That no Blackthorne has divorced in over two hundred years?"

"Believe me, she's not concerned about the family image right now." Trey scrubbed a hand over his head. "That's not what *you're* concerned with when it comes to Mom either."

Brock muttered something under his breath. "Fine. You're right. Would you...would you tell her I'd like her to meet Jenna?"

Jenna Gillespie, the woman who came into his cousin's life because she wanted to write a biography of the Blackthorne family. "I will. She won't be back here for a couple more days, but I'll be sure to pass that on."

"Tell her that I promised Jenna I'd show her how to play bridge and that Aunt Claire is a much better teacher—so we need her back."

"We do," Trey agreed.

"It's not the same without her home," Brock said before ending the call.

Carrying his phone into the kitchen, Trey could only agree with that too. Things weren't the same, and since she'd dropped that word "secret" he'd had this bad feeling they never would be.

He tried shaking off the sense of doom by staring down the coffee-making contraption in the kitchen. But it didn't improve his mood or increase his interest in tackling the unfamiliar device. As he showered and dressed the idea of caffeine persisted however, and he considered knocking on Mia's door and begging, but ignored the urge.

He couldn't ignore thinking about the woman, though. Not to mention why she'd come to Paris. Obviously the loss of her best friend had been a serious blow and he could see she was overwhelmed by the unusual task of taking those ashes about Paris.

His mother had thought he could help with that, which sounded more ludicrous with each passing second. Give him a thorny business negotiation or a thorough read-between-the-lines of a financial statement and he had the experience. The temperament.

But Mia was treading though highly emotional territory and he had it on the authority of women who'd been in then out of his life that he hadn't the heart for it. Knotting his tie, he met his gaze in the mirror and decided he'd send Mia a text and explain he'd been called to the Paris offices.

Once on their premises in the business district known as La Défense, the aide he was usually assigned met him in reception, the main wall painted with the distinctive Blackthorne barrel and thistle logo. Trey apologized for the early hour, which the other man accepted with good grace in his British-tinged, perfect English. To prove himself even more indispensable, Jules placed a cup of coffee in Trey's hand.

With caffeine and a delectable croissant in his system, Trey met with Guillaume and a few others, confirming what he'd said to his father—his visit had been wholly unnecessary. Drinking another cup of excellent coffee, he sat in the third floor break room, his gaze roaming the enlarged photos mounted on the walls that symbolized the family empire—a black and white study of racked casks of whisky, a full-color action photo of one of the B40 racing sailboats, and what could only be called a glamour shot of a stock car with *Blackthorne* emblazoned on the side.

Looking upon those and with the familiar sounds of a workplace in his ears, he leaned back in the chair and mulled over yesterday's meeting with his mother—and not for the first time, though he still couldn't puzzle it out. She'd seemed happy to see him, yes, but there'd been an unmistakable anxiety that caused his own nerves to stand on alert. The night she'd left the King Harbor estate in May she'd been upset and indignant, but yesterday there'd been less evidence of temper and more evidence of...apprehension. There'd been a wariness in her eyes as she seemed to imply she owed an explanation to *him*.

As if Trey was somehow involved in this situation between her and her husband.

"Is something wrong?"

Startled, he glanced over as Jules took the chair beside his. The other man linked his hands on the table. "You're not acting like yourself."

Trey's brows rose. "How's that?"

"You're sitting and doing nothing. You and your father never take the time to savor your coffee, let alone anything else."

The man had a full grasp of the English language...as well as Graham's nature and his own. "An American failing, I'm afraid," Trey said lightly. "Work, work, work. Blackthorne Enterprises is what we can control so we give it our full attention."

And the company was what he'd born and bred to lead. His brother Devlin might poke fun at him, but in a suit and tie

Trey felt the most like himself. Office wear might actually *be* his true skin.

"Time for a change, perhaps? I think the expression is you need to sniff roses, yes?" Jules asked, smiling.

"Smell them," Trey corrected with his own smile. "I guess we haven't found the right incentive."

The other man's gaze shifted over Trey's shoulder. "Perhaps it just walked in," he murmured.

"Huh?" Glancing around, he saw one of the young men who'd sat behind the reception desk ushering a woman thought the glass, logo-etched door.

Both Jules and Trey stood. "Mia?" In boots, jeans, and a yellow long-sleeved T-shirt, with her chestnut hair streaming over her shoulders, she looked bright and casual and...well, lovely. Mouthwatering even, her lips curving though her expression appeared uncertain.

"I hope I'm not interrupting," she said.

The young worker from reception spoke in French so rapid that Trey looked to Jules. "He said he knew you were taking a break so thought he wouldn't leave such a beautiful young lady alone in the waiting area."

Mia showed a full smile at that, her cheeks turning slightly pink as she turned to the young man and thanked him, her French sounding expert enough to Trey.

The kid executed a gallant little bow that only someone from Paris could pull off and then backed out of the room.

Jules reached out his hand to Mia and introduced himself, then told Trey he'd leave the two of them alone. "She smells very nice indeed," he murmured as he passed by. "Better than roses."

When the other man exited the room, Mia bit her bottom lip. "I hope this is okay."

"Didn't you get my text?" Trey asked, slipping his phone from his pocket.

"Yes." She blinked, and he noted the thickness of her curly dark lashes. "You said you'd be tied up for a while at the Blackthorne offices. It's almost noon and I figured I'd come to you and wait around until you were free."

He glanced down at the phone and almost groaned as he realized his text was just as vague as she'd made it sound. His intention had been to drop the news he couldn't partner up for that sightseeing as they'd planned. Maybe when his thumbs had been going at it he'd been thinking of the kiss instead of being clear. In any case, he was thinking of that kiss now, of her sweet mouth and the way her warm body had molded to his.

Then there was the expression on her face when she'd told him why she'd come to Paris. Mia's best friend had passed and the heart he'd been told he didn't have had ached for her loss. Shoving his phone back in his pocket, he glanced out the long windows at the mostly unfamiliar city.

"I guess I'm ready," he said.

Her smile broke over her face and beamed like sunshine over him. "I'm ready too."

A case could be made for their exchange having an ominous undercurrent—readiness implied change and he certainly wasn't eager for that—but he crossed to her anyway. Then she slid her hand in the crook of his elbow.

"Shall we?" she said, with another smile.

And like that…well, somehow he was unsteadied again. His feet too clumsy, his tie too tight, his fingers itching to find hers.

So he did that, covered them where they rested on his forearm, a reassuring and also somehow proprietary gesture.

Disturbingly unlike himself.

And yet, even more disturbing, he didn't regret the touch, nor did he let go of her as they exited the office building and walked into the Paris afternoon.

Stepping onto the sidewalk, understanding dawned on Mia as she considered the surprise, then reluctance, and finally resignation on Trey's face in the office upstairs. Now she belatedly realized he'd thought that morning's text would put an end to their alliance—that he'd meant to renege on the bargain his mother had forced on him the day before.

Gah! Feeling foolish was her most unfavorite thing. She drew in the sun-warmed air and let her hand slip from his arm and drop to her side. He slanted her a quizzical glance. "You don't want this," she said flatly.

He shoved his hands in his jacket pockets, disturbing its perfectly tailored lines. "It doesn't mean I'm not going through with it."

"Trey—"

"I did make that deal with Mom."

Biting her lip, Mia adjusted the strap of the backpack hanging from one shoulder. Inside was her sketchbook and charcoal drawing pencils as well as the box containing Nic's ashes. Part of her wanted to rush back to her basement and hide for another week or two or ten, but another part of her knew if she didn't move now, she'd be mired forever in this inertia.

For herself, she wouldn't mind. But Nic's parents…she knew they truly wouldn't begin letting go without the fulfillment of this promise.

As if sensing her struggle, Trey Blackthorne, the most

handsome man in the city, in the whole world, she thought, took her hand again. "Where to first?"

Okay. She sucked in another breath but freed herself from his hold once more. This had to be done, for Victor and Anne Arsenau. For Nicolette herself. "I have a list."

Can we make it a longer one? Nic's voice asked, gleeful. *Let's draw this out.*

"Let's see it," Trey said. "I'll flag a taxi."

She nearly gasped and then managed to stay his arm as it began to lift. "We're not taking a taxi."

"We're not?"

"Nic wanted the total Paris experience," she said. "That means we take the Métro." The city's subway system was extensive and known for the art nouveau style of the station entrances dating back to the early twentieth century.

She dipped into her pocket and came out with a worn sheet that she'd been carrying around since her decision to go to France.

Over her shoulder, Trey peered at it. "Is that written in code?" he asked.

"Sort of. Nic's version of shorthand. But I know what it says."

"We'll sit down at the nearest café and develop a plan. It makes the most sense to arrange our itinerary geographically."

"Um…" Mia glanced at him. The austere lines of his face and his expensive dark suit made him more than intimidating but she steeled her spine. Despite the fact that his suggestion was no more than common sense, she had to deny him. "We need to do this Nic's way."

His eyebrows rose. "Nic's way? What way is that?"

"It requires an approach of fun and spontaneity."

Trey blinked.

"You've heard of fun?"

Trey blinked again.

"Have you never been spontaneous?" she asked, only half facetiously. Perhaps he'd made every decision using logic and business sense. "It requires—"

"I can be spontaneous," he said, sounding offended. He made to snatch the list from her hand. A rogue burst of wind caught the sheet and it rose into the air, its edges flapping like a bird's wings. They both jumped for it, bumping chests, but it eluded their grasp and floated on the breeze as they ran to keep up with it, dodging bemused pedestrians and stodgy cement planters.

Mia's silent curses turned to out-loud laughter as she watched debonair Trey Blackthorne, half a block ahead, vault over a standard poodle wearing a jeweled collar and then nearly be taken down by the leashes of a pair of little black terriers that wrapped around one ankle.

She had to stop for breath and giggles when a little old lady bopped him with her fresh baguette as he swerved closely around her. But this time he managed to nab the list and he turned to face Mia, expression triumphant, fist raised to the sky.

From her place ten paces away, she brought her palms together in exuberant applause. And like that handsome young Frenchman in the Blackthorne offices, he sketched a bow. The insouciant Parisians did nothing but turn up their noses, which sent Mia into another round of laughter. She jogged up to him, aware of the huge grin on her face, as he wrenched at his tie with his free hand, slipped it from under his collar, then went after his shirt's top buttons.

He looked hot. Both ways.

"Quite the performance," she said. "I'm so impressed." More so with that glimpse of strong neck and throat exposed by the opening of pale cotton fabric. Swallowing hard, she forced her gaze away and held out her hand.

He ignored her silent demand for the list, a new light in his eyes. "Watch how spontaneous I can be." Closing his eyes, his forefinger stabbed the paper. "We're going to…"

"Sacré-Cœur," Mia said, popping on tiptoe to read the scrawled line item. "How appropriate. We'll be starting at the top of the city."

The unexpected chase seemed to change their collective mood. An air of friendly companionship between them, she directed him to the nearest Métro station which took them close to their apartment building so he could change into jeans and a flat-knit, vee-necked sweater. Then they made their way back underground and after two line changes got off at the Abbesses stop. As they came out into open air again, she looked up and noted the beautiful glass-covered "dragonfly" entrance. Tears stung her eyes as she thought of how Nic would have loved the very…Frenchness of the design. "I miss you, best friend," she soundlessly whispered.

"Hey," Trey asked, touching her arm. "Where's that beautiful smile of yours?"

She looked up, her vision filled with his handsome face, her head echoing with that familiar voice that kept Nic so close in her thoughts. *Don't blow this, Mia. Smile at the man.*

So she did, by recalling the baguette-wielder. "I thought I was going to have to save you back there from that little old lady with the loaf of bread."

He grinned. "Me, too. For the first time I'm glad I don't understand French because I think she might have condemned my soul to hell."

"Then you better enjoy the time you have here on earth," she said. "A glass of wine with lunch?"

They found a café among the many on the narrow, hilly

streets of Montmartre, deciding to eat before taking the final climb to the basilica. As she'd come to learn about Paris restaurants, the waiter didn't hurry them along to turn over the table to other guests once they'd eaten, and so they sat in the buttery fall afternoon sunlight, with a second glass of wine in front of each of them.

They talked idly of the surrounding sights, the people passing, and the deliciousness of their simple meal—hearty soup and crusty bread. But now they lapsed into a surprisingly comfortable silence and she studied him as he stared off into the distance, his gaze reflective. The handsome lines of his face were relaxed and without looking her way she saw his mouth curve in a half smile. "You were the one who ordered dessert to share," he said. "If I have some of that tart on my face, you've only yourself to blame."

She wanted to tell him she liked sitting in the warm afternoon with him. That she liked his sprawl in the chair and that she suspected he never allowed himself moments like this. Or his life didn't allow him such moments. But he'd think she was crazy, with her suppositions about who he was and how he lived, she with her box of ashes and with her best friend talking in her head.

"I was thinking of Nicolette," she said, half telling the truth.

He shifted to look at her. "Tell me more about her."

"She was a voice actor. She did commercials, audio books, even video games."

His eyebrows rose. "Really?"

"When she told stories or even spoke of her daydreams, they seemed so real, as if you were right there and everything she imagined was coming true."

He kept his gaze on her face. "I wish I had met her."

"Yes." Then movement behind him caught her attention. "Oh, look!"

A bride and groom were walking up the opposite sidewalk, the young man dapper in a tuxedo, she in enough tulle to wrap the base of the Eiffel Tower. A photographer and assistant accompanied them, laden with bags and cameras.

"Photos at the Sacré-Cœur," their waiter, expression unmoved, said in accented English as he passed by with a tray of empty glasses. "Every day, all day. Very popular."

There was a *mais pourquoi?*—but why?—infusing his bored tone.

Disregarding that, Mia jumped to her feet. "Let's follow them," she said, feeling as if Nic was at her back, her hands propelling her in the wake of the wedding couple.

Without waiting to see if her companion came along, she strode off, scooting around slower pedestrians and stepping into the cobblestone street to avoid shoppers gathered in front of the souvenir shops with their racks of French flags, ubiquitous berets, and plastic replicas of the nearby basilica. Then came a wide walkway with a stone balustrade which finally led to steps. At the top of them sat the imposing, white-domed edifice.

The bride and groom paused at the bottom of the wide stairs and Mia took a seat a few yards away as the photographer and assistant set up the equipment. Trey joined her, stretching out his long legs while she watched the wind catch the young woman's veil and send it swirling into the air.

"They missed a beautiful shot," she murmured, as the groom tried to rein in the swathe of fabric. The wedding couple were laughing as the tulle continued to elude their control.

"Did Nic daydream about her future wedding?" Trey asked, then hesitated. "I hope that's not hurtful."

She shook her head. "It's all right. And no, I don't recall her telling stories about her future wedding day. But she was a bridesmaid a bunch of times. We used to trot out the most hideous of the dresses and wear them while drinking cocktails and alternating between watching episodes of *Sex and the City* and *Game of Thrones*."

His eyebrows shot high. "Really?"

"Good times." She opened her backpack and drew out the handmade box, setting it carefully on the step beside her. "We're here," she whispered.

"What about you?" Trey asked next. "Dreams of white dresses and weddings?"

She made a face. "My parents had a terrible marriage and an even uglier divorce. I think it would take a powerful wizard and a magic spell to make me interested in I do-ing. You?"

"I can honestly say I've never seen myself in a fluffy dress and long veil."

"Hah." She elbowed him. "You've never been married?"

"Nope. Though I wouldn't have said I have anything particularly against it. My parents have been together for thirty-seven years, and happily, I thought. But now..."

"But now you see things differently."

"My father put work first and I've always been exactly like him." He frowned. "At least he took the time to fall in love, though. I know he loves my mother, despite the way he's messed it up."

"But you haven't taken that time to find someone special."

"Obviously not," he said. "I've been much too busy proving I can bear the weight of all the Blackthorne expectations."

"Wow," she said. "One free afternoon and you're deep

into self-psychoanalysis." Though she'd meant it to come out light, almost teasing, the words themselves sounded serious.

He smiled at her. "Actually, it's nothing three brothers and three cousins and numerous friends and disappointed women haven't pointed out over the years. It seems I'm quite predictable."

"Well, that sounds all kinds of wrong," Mia said. "Especially today when we're approaching life with a sense of fun and spontaneity."

"Fun and spontaneity," he repeated.

"Yes. So think of something wild, something totally out-of-character, and we'll do it."

"Yeah?" He cocked a brow.

She nodded, emphatic. "Abso—" But he kissed the rest of the word right off her lips.

Heat flashed through her body and her mind spun. His lips were hard and demanding and she opened her mouth to accept the sure thrust of his tongue. She might have moaned. She definitely moaned when he cupped her face with both his hands and angled her head to make a deeper impression on her.

As if she would, could ever forget being kissed in Paris on the steps to the Sacré-Cœur. But it was his touch that got to her as well, the sureness of the way he held her just so. Just for him. She lost all sense of time and place and everything went…Trey.

Manly Trey. Confident Trey. Kissable, seductive, irresistible Trey.

Teasing Trey, who slowed the kiss by degrees and then lifted his head so she could take breaths that she would have happily foregone for more kissing.

She thought maybe she could exist on his kisses and felt as if she floated on the balmy air.

They stared at each other in that enchanted, autumn light that seemed to sparkle with dancing, gold motes. Her heart pounded and she saw the sheen of moisture on his lips and the flush across his cheekbones. His eyes seemed almost black, impenetrable, except she knew that humor lurked there, as well as all that shiver-inducing self-assuredness.

Not to mention poodle-vaulting.

Hauling in a breath, she felt herself spinning down from the heights, spinning back to her seat on the cement steps. Reality.

She cleared her throat, wondering how to ease the sexual tension pulsing between them. "That wasn't completely unpredictable, you know," she said, trying to sound nonplused instead of soul-shaken. "You've kissed me before."

His smile grew slowly and his gaze never left hers. "And I probably will again."

Without looking away from him, Mia groped for the box of ashes by her side, gripping it for reassurance. *Uh-oh. I might be in trouble here.*

Girlfriend! that Nic-like voice exclaimed, once again filled with glee. *Out of the frozen pond and into the fire. Go you!*

CHAPTER FIVE

TREY COULD HAVE PUT A FINE POINT ON IT AND REMINDED Mia that she'd been the initiator of their first kiss. But he decided to let that detail go—something extremely out-of-character. So was kicking back at a favorite tourist location that was the highest point of the City of Light.

Paris.

Fulfilling a promise of fun and spontaneity.

On a shake of his head, he reached into his pocket for his phone. He should check emails. Better, get back to his mother's apartment, where he'd have more convenient access to files and reports on his laptop. Do some work.

Be himself.

But his hand found the horn box he always carried instead, so he drew it out, aware of Mia's curious gaze. "What's that?" she asked.

He ran his thumb over the top. "It's a container for playing cards and belonged to my grandfather, the first Graham Wallace Blackthorne."

"And you're the third. Trey."

"Right." Their gazes met, held, and then she jumped to her feet, clearly restless. Or nervous.

"Shall we walk again?" she asked. "Get closer to the basilica?"

Standing, he slipped the box away and watched her carefully return the ashes to her backpack. Then she began to climb the stairs, and he followed.

Followed all the way past the milling crowds and the line of visitors waiting to get inside the place of worship to a spot where they had an unobstructed view of the city. It spread before them, buildings crowded together like the decorative pattern of a wide skirt, drawing the eye to the Eiffel Tower rising in the distance.

"It was supposed to be temporary, the Tower," Mia said, her gaze on the landmark. "Many Parisians considered it an eyesore at the time."

"First impressions change."

"Mm." She glanced at him, then gestured to a nearby bench. "Would you mind if I take a few minutes to sketch?"

"Not at all." He could take that same time to look over whatever had come in from Blackthorne HQ. Computing the time change, he realized it was business hours in Boston, meaning his inbox would be stacked.

On the bench, she drew out her sketchbook and pencils and he followed suit with his phone. But he didn't get to work, instead watching from the corner of his eye as her hand began moving over the page.

"Trey?" she asked without looking up. "Now *I* can feel your eyes on me."

"Sorry." He wasn't, because how could he apologize for being fascinated by her? "I remember you said your drawing was private."

"Personal," she corrected. "But you're no longer a

complete stranger. And this view, it's for all to enjoy. I'm only attempting to capture a sense of it on paper."

"You draw buildings or, I guess, landscapes then?"

"People too," she said, then flipped a page and shot him a considering look. "Would you like me to draw you?"

"No," he said, automatically drawing back.

She smiled. "I'll leave your clothes on."

He shook his head.

"Your father then," she offered.

Trey frowned. "You've never met him."

"It's a game we used to play in college. You describe his personality and I draw what I think he looks like."

Intrigued by the idea, Trey couldn't help wondering what she'd come up with. "He's very much like me," he said. "Focused on work, always thinking of the Blackthorne business."

She made a few light gestures with her pencil. "Hobbies?"

"Uh…he used to race forty-foot sailboats with his brother and did it again this summer with my own brother Devlin, but usually he…"

"Focuses on work and is always thinking of the Blackthorne businesses."

"Right."

"He's in his sixties, I suppose." Her hand moved swifter now, but she had her shoulder turned which concealed her progress. "And vacations? Does he have a favorite one? Did he enjoy Hawaii like you?"

Trey thought back to the islands and then the other places they'd gone as a family. His father would invariably show up late and leave early, kind to his boys and their mother while he was present, but usually only paying half-attention to them, engaged in the papers spread before him or with a phone to his ear.

Trey thought of his inbox again and his own phone grew heavier in his pocket. Reaching for it, his gaze caught on Mia's backpack and his mind went to those ashes inside, those ashes of her friend Nic, gone so soon.

You and your father never take the time to savor your coffee, let alone anything else.

"Are you ready to see what I've done?"

"Sure." Shaking himself, he gave Mia his attention.

She kept the sketchbook hidden another moment. "Now keep your expectations low. This is more along the lines of an illustration or caricature, you understand, not a portrait."

"I don't presume a masterpiece," he assured her.

"All right." Shifting on the bench, she presented her drawing.

Startled, Trey stared. The figure portrayed wore a suit and tie and even the simple lines conveyed a sense of tension and movement, as if the man was too busy to stand still. His head was bent over a phone, but the facial features were recognizable…as Trey's own.

She'd drawn an older version of himself. How he'd look at sixty-five, with an overstuffed briefcase at his feet, papers overflowing.

"Well?" Mia prompted. "Did I get it right or wrong?"

"Right…and wrong," he said slowly. "That's Dad to the bone…the way he stands as if ready to stride away to an important meeting in the very next moment. His focus on the phone, that's him too."

"But?"

Trey glanced up. "You've made him resemble me, when the truth is, we don't look alike at all."

"Really?"

"Really." Now he did thumb on his cell and navigated to an old text string from Logan, who'd passed him a couple of photos taken the previous Christmas. Graham and Claire with the seven of the next generation grouped closely around them. "See?"

She took the device and narrowed her eyes at the screen, using two fingers to enlarge the image as she studied the faces. "I do."

He pointed out his brothers and cousins, identifying them one by one. "Devlin, my oldest younger brother who builds boats. This is Philip, the oldest of the cousins who came to live with us when their parents died—he raises money for kids who've suffered the same loss. There's Jason, my cousin who always claims he got lost in the middle but is doing damn fine now as a Hollywood hotshot. Ross, another brother, is into the race cars and whisky side of the business, Brock works at Blackthorne HQ with me in Boston—he's my youngest cousin and a strict keeper of the brand. And finally my little brother Logan, who just moved to Seattle to explore opening some whisky pubs on the West Coast."

She glanced up. "They resemble each other and your father, too, even the cousins."

"Yeah. People see my mom in me, but everyone else has the Blackthorne look."

"Weird how genetics works," Mia mused. Then she flashed him a smile as she returned the phone. "We'd call you a duck with the swans if you weren't already so handsome yourself."

"In any case," he said, ignoring her compliment to indicate the sketch. "You're very talented."

"Does that mean you want me to draw you?"

"Hell, no," he said, the denial automatic. "You're too good. I don't want to see myself through your eyes." But then he hesitated, because damn, he had to admit that image she'd drawn of his father—essentially him, thirty years forward, including briefcase and phone—had unsettled him.

A familiar headache was already throbbing at his temples.

Perhaps she heard the hesitation in his voice or sensed his disquiet. "Give me a chance," she cajoled, flipping the page of the sketchbook. "I may surprise you."

He surprised himself by nodding.

As her hand began to move again, he exchanged his phone for the box of cards. He took them out and began over-hand shuffling them, busying himself while she worked.

The movement soothing, he continued with it, his gaze lifting to the magnificent view. Paris, as he'd never seen it, despite the times he'd been to the Blackthorne international offices in the 8th arrondissement. All business offices felt the same even if they didn't look the same and had better coffee and pastries, he decided. What other parts of the world had he never really, truly seen or appreciated in all his travel for Blackthorne Enterprises that had taken him from the American South to Scotland to Singapore?

More than that, how many years had it been since the family place in King Harbor, Maine, had lost its enchanted kingdom status in his eyes? When was the last time he'd sat down at the property and just…looked at the view of the Atlantic Ocean and lived in the moment, being grateful for all he'd been given through the luck of fate and blood? No wonder his mother had lost her mind at her sixtieth birthday party when she realized that her husband—and by extension, Trey—had turned the celebration of a beautiful life and a toast to its next chapter into an opportunity to further a business deal.

It proved they'd lost their understanding of what was most important, right? But he wasn't sure how to regain perspective—or merely *gain* perspective, he thought with dismay.

"Trey?"

At his name, his hands faltered, and the cards scattered around his feet. He stared down at them, struck by the notion that the universe was slap-in-the-face reminding him he didn't have every aspect of his life under control. That even a Blackthorne could find himself at the mercy of events or people or emotion.

Certainly this trip to Paris proved that, with his inability to corral his wandering mother and her mysterious secret.

"Trey?"

As well as his inability to curb his attraction for one artistic urban mermaid on a mission.

The idea made a man long to smother that knowledge, to run from it by reaching for his cell phone and immersing himself in emails detailing quarterly projections and long-rage strategic plans.

"Trey?"

At the third iteration of his name, he finally looked up. There she was, beautiful, desirable, distracting.

"What do you think?" she asked, and held up her sketchbook.

Transfixed, he gazed on the image she'd wrought with simple pencil strokes. Definitely him, with his short hair and slash of dark brows. But this Trey sat casually, elbows on his knees, his hands loosely linked between them. With a half smile on his face, he stared into the distance, looking faintly bemused and all the way…relaxed.

Content.

A man without the weight of the family mantle on his shoulders.

A man without a care in the world.

A man who wouldn't think about business for the rest of the day and probably for all of the next as well as the one after that.

Hell. He thought he kind of envied that man and…yeah, wanted to be that man too.

The next afternoon, Mia told Trey they needed to wear black for what she had planned for the evening. He stopped on the sidewalk, another paper-wrapped, half-eaten crêpe on its way to his mouth.

The man couldn't get enough crêpes.

His eyes narrowed. "Why?"

She thought about breaking into a little tap dance. Maybe a song. Anything to distract him from that wary look over-taking his face.

Kiss him, Nic said.

Uh, no. No way was Mia going off-task by locking lips once again with the dark-haired, dark-eyed, and totally deli-cious Trey Blackthorne. There was the list to pay attention to, not to mention her innate caution when it came to men. She'd had them in her bed of course, but she'd kept them out of her heart, and instinct told her that her Paris companion could be sneaky that way. Better to double-barricade herself and keep the fooling around limited to *un bisou* or two, already in the past.

What's wrong with more kisses or even a quickie fling?

Mia ignored both questions put to her and pointed across and down the street. "C'mon. See the building topped with the red windmill? That's the Moulin Rouge."

Tourists crowded the sidewalk around the famous building and Trey circled his arm protectively at her waist while she rummaged in her backpack for the box. Silly, she knew, but before she crossed a Paris sight off the list, she brought the ashes into the open air.

Trey peered in the direction of the cabaret's long bank of doors. "Are we going to see a show?"

"No tickets available for tonight," Mia said.

"Let me make a call and perhaps—"

"We have other plans." She didn't need a Blackthorne pulling strings, because cozying up to Trey in a dark venue with half-naked dancers traipsing across the stage might create the wrong mood between them. Though since their kiss at the Sacré-Cœur, he hadn't kissed her again, despite his promise.

She'd deemed her disappointment as ridiculous and decided to be happy enough with his continued companionship. He'd been patient with the lines at the Eiffel Tower and praised the hot chocolate from the famous place on the Rue de Rivoli. A stroll along the shopping avenue of the Champs-Élysées had left them both baffled, since most of the stores were ones that could be found in the States. The Arc de Triomphe impressed them however, bringing to mind images from history and film.

Now she returned the ashes to her backpack and tugged Trey around the corner. She'd done a little homework and knew what she'd find in the Pigalle neighborhood. No longer the den of iniquity it had once been, there were still glimpses of it on the side streets. "We have to get ourselves that black clothing for our evening's adventure," she said.

He took a firm grip of her hand, pulling her close to his side as they passed a sex shop and then a scary looking bar with rough customers standing outside, staring at them narrow-eyed against the bitter smoke from their cigarettes.

At the small mouth of yet another business, she stepped

inside and it opened into a space filled with rows of shelves stacked with folded clothing organized by color.

Used clothing.

She sneaked a peek at Trey, trying to gauge his reaction. He so didn't seem like a previously worn-wardrobe kind of man. "Vintage," she said, lying through her teeth. "It won't take long to find what we need."

According to him, he had a pair of black jeans in his luggage, so they only had to find a black sweater—moth holes no extra charge, the beanpole-sized clerk said, in his peg leg pants and flowered silk kimono—and a black vinyl jacket that surely would insult the French fashion world with its complete inability to pass as leather. She picked up nearly the same, including a pair of pants in dark denim that had ragged hems. To cover her hair, she grabbed a wool beret with a crudely darned rip at the top.

As reward for not insisting they stop at a department store like Le Bon Marché or Galeries Lafayette, she didn't fight too hard over him paying the tab, but stuck some tightly rolled Euros in his back pocket when he reached for the bag on the counter.

"I felt that," he said.

"You're welcome then," she returned with a cheeky smile, and sashayed out of the shop. Then she glanced over her shoulder. "I really am impressed you didn't make a fuss over buying, uh…"

"Used clothes?"

"Well, yes."

He raised a brow. "I seem so snobbish then?"

Devilish, she thought, with that sardonic expression on his face. Still delicious, in the way of dark, near-bitter choco-late. Addicting stuff. "Well, yes," she repeated, hiding behind another sassy smirk. "Or maybe a better word would be stuffy."

"I'm going to wipe that smile right off your face," he murmured, then he had hold of her elbow and towed her inside yet another tight doorway, so quickly she didn't get a chance to take in the signage outside or the display in the dusty front window.

"Eeek." She threw up one hand over her eyes, then immediately brought it down when he whispered, hot in her ear, "Who's stuffy now?"

"I'm no prude," she told him with a frown, and took a slow perusal of the merchandise. Sex-related merchandise. Racks and shelves of potions, lotions, gadgets, devices, and clothing conspicuous for the fabric missing in crucial areas. Though her neck burned with heat, she marched over to one display and held out the first item she grabbed, something with straps and rope and a couple of metal pieces, all shrink-wrapped.

"Shall we buy this, darling?" she asked Trey, innocent as apple pie.

He didn't blink. "What would you say that is, my love?"

"Dear." She gamely gave it a glance. "A badminton net?"

With a shake of his head, he pressed his lips together and then a laugh escaped, and another, until the clerk across the room, with colorful facial tattoos and piercings along the length of his upper lip, sent them a glower.

"We can leave," Trey said, reaching for her hand.

"Absolutely not." Mia avoided him and began a slow browse. "We're in Paris."

"You can find all of this in Paris, Texas," he said. "Or Boston or Tacoma for that matter."

Mia touched a fingertip to a pair of crotch-less panties

hanging on a rack and set the lace swinging. "But here we don't run the risk of bumping into anyone we know."

Trey leaned forward, his mouth to her ear again. "Unless that's Sterling and Isabelle Caine exiting the back room, right under big triple-X in red lights."

His laughter followed her speedy exit from the boutique, and she stood on the sidewalk, glaring at him, hands on her hips. The man had duped her, damn it. "You're mean. And what if that truly had been the Caines?"

"Who would be more embarrassed—them or you? The four of us would be guilty of the same thing after all, if you want to feel guilty over something so harmless."

But what didn't feel harmless was that laughter on his face or the way it warmed her inside. Then there was all that…that merchandise on display that had made her embarrassed and—oh, fine—a little aroused. "We'd better get back to the apartment building," she said quickly, before Nic could start chattering in her head. "We have to rest up for tonight."

At nine p.m. they met in the foyer and set out, she leading the way to the nearest Métro station. Her role as navigator now unquestioned, he kept to her pace without comment. They descended to the tracks, rode a couple of trains to take them outside the city center, and then ascended more stairs, finding themselves on darkened, quiet streets. Looking about, Mia shivered.

Trey put his arm around her waist, and after a moment, she leaned into him.

"Hey," he said, glancing down at her. "What's wrong?"

"Goose walked over my grave," she said automatically, then bit her lip. "By the way, how, um, adventurous are you?"

He pulled her around so she was fully in his embrace, but with inches still between their bodies. His head bent toward hers and the streetlight washed across his handsome features. "What's this about?"

"Um…" She hauled in a breath. "Next question. What's your feeling about cemeteries?" Without waiting for his answer, she described the task ahead.

His fingers tightened on her waist. "You've got to be kidding. Who does that?"

"It's a thing!" she said defensively. "Nic heard it from a friend and read about it on the internet. I researched it too. People do it all the time."

With a groan, he tilted back his head to stare up at the sky, as if seeking aid there. "*Mia…*"

"It's on the list, Trey."

"Have I lost my mind?" he asked, addressing the scattering of stars. "What kind of crazy has she brought into my life?"

His despairing tone awoke her sense of humor. "Oh, c'mon, it's not so bad. I bet there are lots and lots of American women wandering about the city with their BFF's ashes."

"Probably so," he said, in a weary tone. "But how many of them insist on taking said ashes into an old cemetery in order to locate a certain grave statue and then kiss its feet?"

"Rub its wing, I told you," she said, keeping laughter out of her voice with great effort. "It's a fairy and it will bring good luck."

"Good luck," he muttered. "Good God."

"Look on the bright side." She pinned on a winning smile. "This is the only really daring item on the list."

He sighed, then his eyes narrowed. "What else aren't you telling me, wacky mermaid, new plague of my life?"

She decided to leave "wacky mermaid" and "plague of my life" untouched. Maybe it was good he appeared to be irritated with her because his arms around her felt secure and…and…right. Just right.

Clearing her throat, she looked him straight in the eyes. "I don't know what you're so worried about, Mr. Graham Wallace Blackthorne the Third. Surely you can handle anything."

"Appealing to my place in the family won't make me forget about the words 'adventurous' and 'daring.'"

"Please." She rolled her eyes. "Didn't you ever challenge your younger brothers and cousins to feats of bravery? Dare them to, I don't know, see who could hold their breath the longest underwater or keep their hand over a candle flame?"

"I warned them against passing out and stood on watch if rescue was needed," he said without expression. "And if they played with fire, I told my mother."

It was too much. Mia burst out laughing. "That does it. It's absolutely imperative that we break into the cemetery and find that statue. You definitely need to bend some rules."

Then she slipped from his hold to scamper off, hearing him curse followed by the thud of his footsteps in her wake.

"Break into the cemetery?" he stage-yelled.

She smothered another snort of laughter and kept on running.

But it wasn't as bad as all that. Because it couldn't really count as breaking in, and she told him so, as she stopped beside the gap in the memorial park's surrounding iron fence, just as had been described on the Graveyard Groupies website. Here, one of the twisted pickets had been somehow bowed toward its neighbor, leaving a space large enough for a body to slip through easily.

Her body, anyway.

Trey's emergence into the burial grounds required quite a bit more maneuvering. Plus a few quiet curses.

"You did it," she finally said with muted exuberance, patting his arm. "You made it look easy."

He tugged on the bottom of his cheesy jacket and even in the darkness she could feel his quelling look. "My mom loved the game Twister."

Before she could start laughing at the idea of dignified Trey Blackthorne willingly pretzeled, she murmured, "Right foot, green," and started off in the direction indicated by the instructions she'd downloaded to her phone. She used the flashlight function to illuminate their way and they passed headstones and raised crypts and crosses of all designs. There were statues here and there as well, angels and saints being a popular choice, but none the one they sought.

A rustling in a nearby shrub made her jump and Trey laid a steadying hand on her shoulder. "Don't chicken out on me now," he said. "I'm establishing some serious street cred with this caper."

She barely managed to smother her snort and gamely carried on. Right here, left there. Past the soldier on a horse and beyond the headstone shaped like a cello. Then, finally, she saw the fairy. Like something from an art nouveau illustration, it was human-sized and standing on a twelve-inch-high column, with a willowy form, a serene expression, and outstretched wings.

"Beautiful," she breathed. Really, it was, the lines delicate, the folds of its gown lifelike and the figure's flowing hair twined with tiny leaves and blossoms.

Gripping Trey by the arm, she pointed. Before they could make a move though, a pair of teens darted out from behind a nearby crypt, their excited voices carrying in the night. Crap, she thought, slipping her phone with its betraying light into her pocket. There were guards on the prowl all night long, according to the website. It advised extreme quiet.

"*Shh*," she whispered, but they either didn't hear her or paid her no mind. More likely, they were adolescents and thus wholly absorbed in themselves.

The kids cavorted closer to the statue while she and Trey stayed in the shadows under a pine tree. The giggling pair finally got close enough to run their hands over one wing, then they embraced with a fervency that made Mia blush. It was only worse when they began kissing ravenously and she dropped her head as Trey whispered in her ear, "And for extra good fortune, be sure to inhale each other's tonsils."

She clapped her hands over her lips and kept them that way until she heard the departure of the couple. "Whew," she whispered.

"Yeah," he agreed. "I was just about to yell 'get a room.'"

That tickled her funny bone and she swallowed another snort even as she approached the statue and slipped her backpack off her shoulder. With the small box of ashes in one hand, she stroked the edge of the angel's wing with the other, finding the marble worn where she imagined hundreds of others had sought the rumored outcome.

"You next," she whispered to Trey as she returned the box to its nest and resettled her backpack.

"Not me," he said. "I'm not superstitious. I don't believe in magic."

With a shake of her head, she grabbed him and guided him firmly toward the lovely figure. Mia linked their hands and lifted them to the swoop of marble. She held his there, sandwiched by hers, and then somehow their fingers were tangled and she was standing close to his back, nestled against him, the two of them as one.

The marble seemed to vibrate beneath their touch. Mia sucked in a breath, held it, and then Trey glanced over his shoulder at her face. The night went still.

Her heart beat slowly, but she thought his must beat in the same rhythm, the two of them, alive in this moment. In sync.

Oh, no. The words whispered in her mind, but they were her very own this time. Her own instincts expressing dismay.

Yet she didn't move. The night closed around them like a velvet cloak, providing a private place for a private moment between two people who might never have met and yet who had, despite their differences. And despite every reason against it, she'd never felt this close to any other man.

Then an angry French voice shot out of the darkness. Mia stiffened and a flashlight arced over their surroundings, once, twice, only to hone in on the two of them like a spotlight. Trey whirled to face the threat, pushing her behind his bigger body.

She peered around his arm to see a hulking presence in the uniform of a security guard. He spoke rapidly, too quick for her to understand though his meaning was quite clear regardless. They were where they shouldn't be.

To confirm it, she caught a word in the barrage of rebukes. *Gendarmerie.* Police.

Mia ducked around Trey, stepping into the harsh light. "Sir," she said, trying to gather her thoughts in a second language. "Sir. Please. *S'il vous plaît.*"

Additional French words escaped her, her vocabulary evaporating.

So she resorted to English. "I'm sorry. You see, we need the luck. My lover," she glanced back at Trey, "we're meant to be together. Fated. But his family, you see they don't understand we're soul mates, and we need the…the…*bonne fortune.*" The phrase for good luck tumbled off her tongue.

"Just introduce us as Romeo and Juliet and get it over with," Trey grumbled.

"The French love lovers," she said out of the side of her mouth.

"Everybody loves extra cash in their pocket," he countered, and produced some folded Euros that he held out to the man.

After a moment's hesitation, the charged atmosphere changed from hostility to downright bonhomie. The handful of cash bought them an actual smile and then an escort by flashlight out the main entrance.

With a wave for their new pal, by tacit agreement they returned directly to the apartment building—this time by taxi. In the foyer, Trey pulled more bills from his pocket and fanned them in front of her. "What will it take to get you to make a couple of cups of my mother's coffee?"

"Put your money away," she said, and marched for the elevator. "I don't accept bribes."

Upon reaching the penthouse apartment, she set aside her backpack and they both stripped off their fashion-backward jackets. Then he followed her into the kitchen and watched her use the French press to make two steaming cups. After a short rummage in a cupboard, he discovered a packet of small cookies.

As she slid his coffee along the countertop toward him, he narrowed his eyes at her. "Okay, what's up? Something's happened. What's bugging you?"

Could she be truthful? Could she tell him she was desperate to gin up some dissatisfaction with him, some way to forget how all evening he'd been both fun and funny? The consummate co-adventurer.

Then there was that...that...togetherness, when they stood, body-to-body with barely a breath between them, touching the statue.

"You could at least blame me for getting threatened with arrest," she said, her tone sulky.

For some maddening reason he seemed to find that amusing. "Well, it *is* somewhat disappointing that I didn't have to call Devlin or Brock and beg to get bailed from jail in Paris because of...what would we have been taken in for exactly? Unlawful fondling?"

"There wasn't any 'fondling.'"

He lifted his cup and met her eyes over the rim. "To my everlasting regret."

Bad man! "Don't go getting flirty with me," she said, frowning and scurrying back to put two feet between them. "Be angry or annoyed or something helpful like that."

His lips twitched. "I do have one complaint."

"What's that?"

"You owe me some skin."

The hand holding her own coffee arrested on its way to her mouth. "Huh?" Her flesh prickled beneath her second-hand clothes. Was that some gambit to get her naked? "What do you mean exactly?"

He set his beverage down and began to lift the hem of his sweater, taking the white undershirt he wore beneath with it. "I mean I left behind an inch or two of mine crawling through that fence."

"No," she breathed, and dropped her cup to the counter on her way to getting closer to him. "Let me see," she demanded, but he grabbed her hands and yanked her toward him instead.

With an *oomph*, she landed against his chest and then he was kissing her, his lips still cold from their nighttime activities, but his mouth hot, so hot, from the coffee and from whatever impulse made him eager to kiss her again.

"I've been wanting to do that all night," he murmured,

and she abandoned herself to her own desires, kissing him back, her body as flush to his as she could make it.

He groaned, his hands sliding down her back to cup her bottom and tilting her hips so his heavy shaft rocked against her at a place that made her moan. She opened her mouth to the deep thrust of his tongue and she parried with her own, teasing too.

Lifting his head, he groaned again. "You do something to me. A spell."

Her mouth trailed along his jawline, prickly with whiskers and she thought of how they might feel elsewhere, on the inside of her elbow, on the outer curve of her breast. "You don't believe in magic."

"If anyone could make me change my mind..." He found her mouth for yet another kiss, lavish and lascivious and so fiery it put the teenagers' fumblings to shame.

This time, she broke free to haul in a breath. "You're good at this."

He grinned, and lifted her onto her toes with a boost at her butt. His mouth dropped a peck on her nose. "I take it you don't object?"

God, she liked this playful version of him, so different than the tired businessman who'd stepped out of the taxi that first day. She threw her arms around his neck, tugging him down to trace his mouth with the tip of her tongue. A tremor coursed through his body, sending a flash of heat over hers. It was heady stuff, to know she affected him as much as he affected her.

He took over again, his lips hard and his tongue demanding and she let herself be led wherever he wanted to go, thrusting her breast into his hand as it slid beneath her sweater and cupped her there.

His thumb passed over the crest and she quivered, her

head dizzy with a building desire. Dampness rushed between her thighs and she shoved her fingers into the back of his short hair, the strands like mink against her skin. Then he pinched her nipple and she gasped, her body jerking, more wetness gathering at the juncture of her legs.

Her nails dug into his scalp and he lifted his head, his gaze burning into hers. "Mia." His throaty voice was like a stroke down her spine.

She shivered again. "Yes?"

"What do you want to do about this?"

To avoid his eyes, she rested her forehead against his chest, feeling the steady, heavy thud of his heartbeat. "Um... how about you?"

He moved back, putting space between them, both of his hands moving to the relatively safe zone of her waist. "I like you, Mia Thomas. I don't want to hurt you or play with your feelings."

"I don't want to hurt you either," she said, looking up, and decided upon pure honesty. "But...but I do want you, Trey Blackthorne."

"For this moment?"

She nodded. "For this moment. No thought about anything but now. No concerns for the future. Or thoughts about the past."

"Or thoughts about the past," he repeated, like a promise.

Then, grinning in what seemed to be perfect accord, they moved into each other again. Her blood ignited, her belly tightened in sweet anticipation.

The sound of a key in the front lock acted like a dousing pail of cold water.

CHAPTER SIX

TREY'S HEAD SHOT UP AND HE LOOKED TOWARD THE NOISE AT the entrance to his mother's apartment. "No," he said. It couldn't be. Not since his little brother Logan had burst into their King Harbor boathouse when Trey had been hoping to reach second base with Natalie Schroeder had he been so thwarted.

And so frustrated.

Muttering a curse, he put Mia from him and ran both hands through his hair, smoothing any disorder and willing his pulse to calm and his hard-on to subside. "Mom?" he called out. "Is that you?"

His gaze flicked to his kitchen companion to see that she was straightening her clothes. Then her hand went to her coffee and eyes on him, she lifted it for a hefty swallow.

"All good?" he asked in a low voice.

She nodded, her gaze filled with both regret and amusement. "I haven't felt sixteen since...well, sixteen."

He grinned, then couldn't help but reach out and cup her cheek. His thumb stroked a line over the cinnamon dust of freckles there. "Rain check?"

Her lashes swept down. "Oh, I—"

"Oh, I owe you," he said and felt her answering smile as well as saw it. "More kisses, Mia. More…everything."

"If you're sure—"

"Yes." Her skin had heated beneath his touch and his blood chugged southward again. "I'm so damn sure." Another rustle from the front of the apartment snagged his attention, and before he forgot where he was in the pleasure of who he was with, he called out a second time. "Mom?"

"It's me," Claire said.

"You're back early." He forced himself away from Mia and out of the kitchen, wondering if his mother had lost her uncanny knack of knowing when one of her boys was up to mischief.

She didn't even glance at him, though, as she fussed with her roller bag and parcels.

"Let me help," he said, striding forward to draw a large soft-sided tote from under her arm.

"My art portfolio," she murmured, then began unwinding her blue scarf, its edges decorated with flowers and leaves that he thought she might have done herself—he vaguely recalled her with that fabric in hand along with a needle and thick thread. "Be careful with it."

"Of course I will." He set it atop the table beside the door. "Did you run into a problem?"

"No, no." His mother didn't meet his gaze. "Our instructor learned that a villa in Ghent has come available. We've decided to go there for a few days and we're scheduled to leave from the Gare du Nord in the morning."

"In the morning?" He frowned. "Mom, you can't just run out on me again—"

"We'll have our talk," she said. "I promised you and I promised myself."

"Hi, Claire." Mia strolled in from the kitchen. "I've just put on the kettle to brew some of that tea you like so much."

His mother brightened. "I'm so happy to see you, honey." She shot a glance at Trey. "Does this mean you two have been..."

"Sightseeing," he put in. "I've kept to my part of the bargain."

"Right, right." Her smile appeared forced. "You'll have to tell me all the places you've visited."

"Mom." Trey sighed. "Can we just get this over with? Have our conversation without any more stalling?"

Her hands came together at her waist. "Yes. We should." She glanced at Mia.

"I'll go," the younger woman said, already on the move.

"I'd love that tea, though," Claire said quickly. "Do you mind?"

Mia reversed direction. "Of course. I'll be right back."

Trey took his mother's elbow in a gentle grasp and led her into the living room. They both took seats on one of the light green couches. The night seemed to press in from the large windows and he stood to turn on more lights.

Looking worried, Mia brought in a tray of cups and saucers and those cookies he'd found on a small plate. Claire took her tea with a grateful smile. Trey lifted his coffee and swallowed a fortifying sip.

"Now I'll go," Mia said. "It's good to see you again, Claire."

The older woman reached out a hand. "Might you stay? I could use...a friendly face."

"Mom." Trey stared at her, aghast. "I'm the enemy now?"

"Of course not. It's just..." She looked down at her cup.

He shot a glance at Mia, feeling up against a wall. "Do you mind joining us?"

With another worried glance at his mother, she shook her head then took a seat on an adjacent chair.

Trey returned to his place. "Out with it, Mom. What's this big mystery?"

She pulled in a long breath. "First…first you should know that your father and I love you very much."

His heart slammed against his ribs, his mind leaping to a conclusion. "Are you ill?"

"No." She shook her head.

"Dad? I know he's supposed to be watching his cholesterol—"

"No."

"Well, I know *I'm* fine. All the Blackthorne executives had physicals three months ago."

His mother's smile appeared genuine now. "Yes. That was good to have confirmed, of course, though you've never been sick beyond the usual colds."

"I come from good stock. Look at how hale Nana is at eighty-six. Blackthornes age well."

The tea cup rattled as his mom set it in the saucer, her skin paling.

Unsure what else to do, Trey tried lightening the heavy atmosphere. "Though there was that time I broke my tailbone falling down the stairs during flashlight tag. Dev proved early to be a pain in my ass. You and Dad should have stopped at one son instead of four."

His mother looked up, her expression anguished. "We meant to. We thought we'd only have the single child."

Trey forced out a chuckle. "I won't have that conversation with you, Mom. I shouldn't have to, because I believe it was you who presented that very odd book to explain the process to me when I was eight. It starred gophers, if I recall correctly."

She didn't laugh.

"Mom." He pushed both hands through his hair. "What the hell is it?"

"Thirty-five years ago was a different time." She set aside her cup and saucer, then folded her hands together, knuckles whitening. "So many technologies were new, so many others not even dreamed of yet. Now I read they catch criminals using DNA and extended family trees."

"In case you're thinking of the rumored whisky bootlegging," Trey said, "even if it is true, the statute of limitations would have run out by now."

She looked up, clearly distracted. "What?"

"Jason can tell you that whole story when you come home." He paused. "You *are* coming home?"

"This…what I have to tell you is separate from that. Or mostly separate from that."

Trey shot a look at Mia, though he didn't know why. He doubted she understood what was going on either. Then he focused back on his mother. "All right. To recap. New technologies, new criminal detection capabilities."

"We went to the very best clinic. All the way across the country in Washington State. And they recommended we keep it a complete secret."

"A clinic?" Trey couldn't puzzle it out. No one was sick, she'd said.

"Thirty-five years ago, we paid for exclusivity and were assured of complete confidentiality."

He stilled. *Thirty-five years ago.* The first real clue.

"You see, your father didn't want anyone to know there was a fertility issue at all and especially that the doctors determined the problem was his."

"What?"

His mother shifted uncomfortably. "Very few, uh, swimmers. And low motility, they said."

"*What?*" Low sperm count, a fertility clinic across the country. The pieces were starting to come together. "This is about, well, me?"

"Yes." Mom looked down. "About you."

"Are you saying I was conceived in a petri dish?" He didn't know much about the process of...IPF? No, IVF. It had to have been a fairly new procedure at the time.

Her gaze moved up to his. "So to speak. And I've been worrying and worrying about not telling you since forever, but especially once those home DNA tests cropped up. My friend Dora Madigan's son-in-law, you know the one, Geordie Browne, who went to DC to do something secret for the government? He has that limp leftover from an auto accident, and you barely notice it, but Dora says—"

"Mom, I don't know this Geordie Browne, and at this moment I don't care about him either. What the hell are you trying to tell me?"

"Geordie Brown's father had a fling during college and got a girl pregnant. He has a sister he never knew about—until he took a test that his wife gave him at Christmas. For fun. They merely were curious to find out if he was truly part Sicilian."

Trey rubbed at his forehead, trying to process. Sicilian-or-not Geordie he discarded as irrelevant. "Are you saying Dad had a college fling? That we have a sister? And that you and Dad needed help getting pregnant with me?" He pressed his fingertips to his skull. "I'm not following."

"Just the last," his mom said. "We needed help getting pregnant with you and thirty-five years ago we visited a fertility clinic." She paused to take a long breath. "Where my egg was, um, fertilized by anonymous donor sperm."

Silent, Trey replayed the essential bit in his head. *My egg was fertilized by anonymous donor sperm.* "Say that again," he finally said.

"My egg." Mom cleared her throat. "And donor sperm."

He continued attempting to wrap his head around it. So he hadn't misheard? "Not Dad's sperm? Not Blackthorne sperm?"

She nodded.

"The four of us, me, Devlin, Ross, and Logan, we're not biologically Dad's sons."

Looking at him with a combination of anguish and sympathy, she pressed her lips together. "Just you, honey. Miracle, misdiagnosis, whatever the case, your father's condition changed. Your brothers are his and conceived in the, uh, usual manner."

The inside of his head went quiet. So quiet. "But me, I'm someone else's son."

Her expression turned fierce. "You are mine and you are your father's, Graham's," she said, her tone vehement, "in every way that matters."

We'd call you a duck with the swans, Mia had told him, upon noting how unlike his looks were to his brothers and cousins.

I'm someone else's son.

The room took a seasick spin, as if the world had lost its axis.

"We wanted children so badly," his mother said. "And I can't tell you how over the moon we were to find out the procedure was a success."

Trey had seen photos of his mother at various stages of pregnancy with him, beaming, Graham's arm securely around her. Graham in the delivery room. Graham holding infant Trey, the son that wasn't his.

"You should have told me." His voice sounded rusty.

"They advised us not to." The look on her face implored him to understand. "They were the best in the country and we listened to them because they were the experts. The ones we trusted to help us gain the thing we wanted most of all."

We'd call you a duck with the swans.

I'm someone else's son.

Trey rose, though he couldn't feel his legs. "I'm going for a walk."

His mother held out her hand. "Sweetheart, please…"

"I need fresh air so I'm going for a walk."

From the corner of his eye, he saw Mia stand too. "Alone."

Mom bit her lip. "Are you sure?"

"I'm sure." It was perhaps the only thing he was certain of in his life—that he needed to get out of the room, this apartment, and into the cold night air of a strange city.

Apt, for a man who was now a stranger to himself.

"We'll talk more as soon as you're ready," his mother said quickly. "I'll stay right here until you get back, or if you'd rather, in the morning—"

"Don't wait up, Mom," he said, already moving toward the front door. "And go to Ghent as planned."

"I can't do that," she said, forehead pleating.

"Yes, you can. Please do it. Please do it for me."

"Trey—"

"Now *I* need some time, Mom." He couldn't begin to imagine what more he had to say to her when he couldn't think beyond…beyond…

We'd call you a duck with the swans.

I'm someone else's son.

Mia lay wide awake in bed when a light knock sounded on her front door. She bounded off the mattress, as sure as she knew her own name the identity of the person on the other side.

The man whose own identity had been shaken hours earlier.

Her throat tightened, her chest squeezed, and her footsteps paused, as she was struck by the enormity of what Trey must have been going through. What could she possibly say in the face of that? Maybe she should pretend sleep and avoid him altogether.

Because what gave her the idea she could help him in any way? Perhaps he would resent her assumption that she could.

Yet she was already on the move again, something propelling her toward him, the same force she'd felt when they'd been touching the fairy's wing together. As if they'd found themselves in Paris for just this—a moment under the stars and another in the early hours, both of them needing a companion through unfamiliar emotional terrain.

With her hand on the doorknob, she hesitated again. She'd never, not once, had a relationship with a man that involved this kind of intimacy.

For goodness' sake, open the door! Nic urged. *Your guy is hurting.*

The disquieting "your guy" Mia ignored, and she swung open the door to find Trey standing there, his hands in the pockets of the terrible faux-leather coat, his handsome features faintly reddened with cold. "Come in, come in," she said, scooping her hand to encourage his entry.

Instinct told her not to touch him. He looked nothing like the harried businessman checking his phone she'd spied that first day nor did he bear much resemblance to the good-humored sightseeing companion she'd come to know. Those dark eyes of his weren't tired or amused, but lost.

"Come *in*," she said again, and this time he obeyed, only to stand in the middle of her living area, blinking as if surprised to find himself in her place. Then he turned his gaze on her, as if surprised to find her there, too.

"Are you all right?" she asked, wondering where he'd been.

"About an hour ago I found an all-night bakery," he said.

She glanced at the clock. Almost five a.m. "I think it probably opens very early in the morning."

"I bought a baguette." He brandished the long loaf in one hand.

"Are you hungry?"

He shook his head. "It was for self-defense. The neighborhood about a half-mile south of here isn't all that good."

"You were going to keep yourself safe with bread?"

For a moment he seemed to consider it. "I wasn't thinking clearly."

"Right." She opted for a brisk tone. "Do you want coffee?"

"No." He hesitated. "How was my mom when you left her?"

"Okay. Tired. I helped her pack for her next trip and then she said she was going to bed."

"Thank you." With another baffled look around, he gestured with the baguette. "I interrupted your sleep."

"I think you need some." She took the loaf from his hand and crossed to her kitchen area to put it on the counter. "Would you like to stay here?"

He nodded.

"Okay." Briskly, she crossed to the small cabinet that

stored extra linens and pulled free a stack. "I'll make up the sofa."

His dubious look at the piece of furniture said what he didn't have to.

"I'm on the sofa," she told him, snapping a sheet straight. "You'll get my bed."

"Mia…"

He'd tossed his jacket aside and stood in the moth-eaten sweater, with its glimpses of white cotton through the holes, reminding her of the stars in the night sky they'd seen earlier. For her, he'd risked liberty and dignity to sneak into that cemetery. Surely she could offer a sympathetic ear.

"Do you want to talk?" she asked, tossing a pillow and blanket onto the cushions.

His hand slipped into his pants pocket and he pulled out that box of cards, looked at it, then slipped it away again.

That had been his grandfather's, she remembered, her chest tightening once more. The first Graham Wallace Black-thorne. God, how upended he must be feeling about now. "I might not guarantee I have any answers or certainly the right ones, but I'll listen."

He looked down. "No thanks. I'm good."

She hoped the relief coursing through her didn't show on her face. Keeping her relationships with men friendly but shallow had maintained her heart-whole status and it didn't take a couch and a box of tissues in a therapist's office to know that her parents' ugly divorce had made her averse to any action or any man that might threaten that.

Trey threatened everything, her instincts knew. Best to keep to friendly and shallow than to dive into something deep and scary. Her mother said that she and Mia's father had never been in love and their daughter could only decide it was true, because true love couldn't turn into disrespect, despair, and disaster, especially when a nine-year-old was smack dab in the middle of that marriage.

So she didn't know what the heck romantic love would look and feel like. Because of that, Mia deemed it best to keep clear of thinking in that direction in case some imposter emotion tried shouldering its way in and cause a very real danger.

Trying to appear upbeat and matter-of-fact, she made to brush past him. "Let me just get my phone and then the bedroom is all yours."

But once inside the small space, she turned to realize he'd followed her, making her suddenly aware of what she wore as nightgear—a pale pink vintage slip she'd picked up at one of the Paris flea markets. It was probably from the 1930s, with lace at the vee of the bodice and around the hem that landed not indiscreetly somewhere between her behind and her knees. It wasn't particularly racy, not really, but her heart was racing all the same as she took in the way that Trey's gaze seemed to burn right through the thin silk.

Nic's voice sounded in her head, amused and excited. *Mia, this is—*

"Shut it," she murmured to her friend.

Shutting it. Going away.

Her feet rooted to the spot, Mia watched Trey approach. That lost look in his eyes had turned to heat and when his hands landed on her shoulders, they were hot too, transmitting enough fire to speed her blood and bring up goose bumps on her arms, legs, and everywhere in between. His gaze, however, was fixated on her mouth.

"Mia," he said, his voice husky. "Beautiful Mia."

She sucked in a deep breath and felt her nipples peak against the delicate fabric covering them. Her hands went to his waist, but he reached down to grip her wrists and bring them up to circle his neck. He moved in, his big body brushing hers.

"Do you know what you're doing?" she whispered.

One corner of his mouth kicked up. "Being spontaneous." His hands slid down her arms and then he wrapped his arms around her body, pressing her flush against him.

Her eyes closed as his head bent over hers. "What did we say earlier?" he asked. "No thoughts about the past?"

Ah. So she would be his path to forgetfulness, she thought, willingly opening her mouth as he took hers in a deep, needy kiss. Her fingers slid through the short hair at the back of his neck a cool pelt in contrast to the burning, consuming flame that leaped in her chest as their lips pressed together and his tongue thrust to rub against hers.

She shivered, shimmying against his hard frame, and his hands slid down to cup her bottom, then moved lower as he fisted the slip and drew it up and over her head. As he tossed it away, she considered what to do with herself, clad only in tiny panties and nothing else. But then his gaze ran over her and any chill she might have felt, any apprehension that might have cooled her blood was gone, and she reached for his sweater and took his undershirt too, getting him half-naked as well.

Kisses came next. Fast and greedy, slow and drugging, with the metal of his belt buckle pressed to her stomach, a brand she willingly bore and could almost hope would show still tomorrow. Marked by Trey, proof that she'd let go and been touched and taken and touched and taken in return. Proof that for a night, at least, she'd mattered to this beautiful man.

Then he was on his knees, his mouth on her belly and her hip bones, lower. Her skin burned with the embarrassment of it, but that awkwardness lasted only a few moments until he slipped her panties off. His tongue worked its way into the cleft of her sex and passed over the knot of nerves there, stroking, circling, sucking. Her head fell back, her fists at her sides while one of his hands kneaded the round cheek of her bottom and his other thumbed her more open for his wet, velvety caresses, making her take every delicious stroke.

With a moan she lost it, an unexpected climax seizing control of her, causing more moans and shivers and a loss of any awareness save that of Trey. Handsome Trey, skilled Trey, wicked Trey who stared up at her as his mouth soothed now instead of incited. Her heart pounded in her chest, toes, fingertips, and throat, and when he laid her on the bed, she opened her arms and legs and invited him close again.

Eyes on her body, he threw off the rest of his clothes, tossing them onto the straight chair. Though arousal began to rise again as she took in his long, muscled limbs and the heavy thrust of his flushed sex, wisdom prevailed. "Condom?" she asked, her voice throaty.

"Someplace was open all night," he answered, as he leaned down to fish in the pocket of his pants. For a moment she thought it might be his phone, then he pulled out a foil packet. "The condom dispensers outside the pharmacies."

Maybe she would have made some teasing comment about his over-confidence but whatever it might have been was lost when he came over her, his heat and scent so good, so natural. She shifted her legs so he was cradled by her hips and then he was kissing her again, like her kisses were what he'd been waiting for all his life.

He kissed her chin and down her throat and then moved to her breasts. She arched upward, asking for more, and he gave it in the arousing sting of tiny bites until he sucked on her nipples, sensation arrowing to her sex, making her cry out, telling him her body was ready, willing, eager to be penetrated by him, for them to be connected like under that starry sky.

She begged, pleaded, ordered, used the edge of her nails to make her wishes known and he groaned at that last. "God, you make me wild," he said. The condom he'd tossed to the bed was found, she insisted on rolling it on, clumsy with lust, so he had to take over, laughing.

Then neither of them made a sound as he slowly came inside her, hovering over her body with an elbow on each side of her, his eyes trained on hers as he drove with powerful, steady strokes. The room was the muted gray of dawn, smudging the details of everything in it except Trey—solid Trey, sexy Trey, the master-of-her body Trey.

They came, one after the other, in near silence, the only sound their heavy breathing. His face against the side of her neck, his weight pressing hers to the mattress, he recovered for long minutes, then he lifted his head to look at her.

She stared back, wishing to avert her eyes but caught by something in his she couldn't name. "I think…" he started, then dropped kisses to her brows and her nose and finally her chin.

"I hate when people start a sentence and then drop it," she said, sounding cranky, because she was desperate to know his thoughts and wasn't that a disaster just in itself?

"I love your sulky mouth," he said, kissing her there, soft and quick.

"Tell me," she demanded, her hands gripping his broad shoulders. He was still inside her, she could feel him there, but then she thought she might always feel him there.

More disaster!

"You think…what?" she tried again, going for winsome.

His smile grew like the sunrise, basking her in light and heat. "I think we should have a Paris fling."

CHAPTER SEVEN

TREY SAT ON THE COUCH IN MIA'S LIVING AREA, HIS PHONE to his ear, as his call connected to Greg Tulley, head of Tulley Investigations in Laguna Beach, California.

"I've been expecting to hear from you," the other man said.

"Yeah." Trey checked a nearby clock, realized that nine a.m. meant it was midnight Pacific time, and grimaced. "Late for you, though. Sorry."

"Not a problem."

Still, Trey decided he'd add a bonus to the hefty bill Greg would surely send for the rush job he'd requested last night from a bench along the Seine river. Then it had been heading toward midnight in Paris, but still business hours on the West Coast of the United States. Not for a minute did he doubt that Greg hadn't already found something to report.

Though Trey could have turned to the security head of Blackthorne Enterprises, a woman in whom he had complete trust, he'd decided to call Greg for this. They'd used the former Navy intelligence officer in the past when someone threatened, via regular mail postmarked in Southern California, to burn down the original whisky distillery in Maine. The culprit turned out to be a bored and basically harmless seaman based in San Diego with an overblown allegiance to the brand of spirits made in his Kentucky hometown. Greg had tracked him down and after a chat with the kid and his commanding officer, the problem had been neutralized.

But during the investigation, both Trey and Brock had spoken with Greg and developed a confidence in the private detective as well as a genuine liking for him. So last night, reeling from the new knowledge imparted by his mother, Trey had decided to contact the other man. As expected, he'd taken the assignment with professional aplomb and with the promise he'd immediately get to work on the issue.

"What can you tell me?" Trey asked now.

"First, some background."

"All right." Though he'd done a little basic research himself the night before, again from that bench along the river, he'd listen to what Greg had to say.

"The first baby born through IVF is over forty years old," the other man told him. "It's now done all over the world and there are various regulations for it and for sperm donation as well."

"In the US?" Trey thought he knew the answer.

"In the US there are no rules about who may donate sperm. Private expert groups offer recommendations, but there is no enforcement of guidelines or any sort of tracking."

"What did you find out about the specific clinic my mother used?"

"I think I know which one it is…pretty simple detective work given the year you provided and the relative newness of the procedure at the time. I called and they confirmed they offer completely anonymous donorship and that exclusivity is available…for a very hefty fee."

"Of course. But price would have been no issue for my mother and…" *Hell.* Pain sliced through his head. "For my mother and Graham."

"A member of my staff made another call," Greg continued, "posing as someone who recently learned they were conceived at that clinic and fathered by an unknown donor."

Trey pressed a hand to his temple. "Posing as someone like me."

"Yes." Greg's businesslike tone somewhat lessened the ache in Trey's head.

"And?" he prompted.

"Just as advertised, they were steadfast in their refusal to provide any information." He hesitated. "Even when money was offered."

"A bribe," Trey said.

"An incentive." Greg cleared his throat. "But neither the person she spoke with on the administrative staff nor a doctor she insisted on speaking to next expressed the slightest inclination to exchange information for cash."

"All right."

"And my staffer was good, but nothing moved them," Greg added. "I assure you she pressed. There were tears, but no go. Anger didn't work either."

Anger. Until this moment, Trey had managed to keep his at bay, but it rose from his gut now, closing off his throat. What had been the damn plan? Claire and Graham, the two of them keeping this secret to the grave?

"Trey." Greg's voice lowered. "Are you doing all right?"

He realized he'd squeezed the phone as if to strangle it. With deliberate intent, he relaxed his fingers on the device. Then he drew in a calming breath and let it out to ease the constricting band that had been tightening around his chest since he awoke in bed, next to Mia. "I'm great," he said, thinking of her, those warm limbs that had twined with his in sleep.

"You should know about a donor's rights too."

His chest tightened all over again. This hadn't occurred to him—that the person who provided the half of his DNA he didn't know about might be entitled to…what? "Greg, I—"

"In this case, the donor's parental rights and obligations are waived. Completely. Irrevocably. Attitudes are changing in respect to this and to anonymity, but you don't have to worry about someone popping up claiming to have fathered the scion of the Blackthorne family."

"Good," Trey said. But hell, was it good? Part of him was a great void now, his sense of identity…

The remainder of that thought evaporated as Mia drifted into the living area, her hair rumpled and her delectable body wrapped in a floral robe that even now she was tying at the waist. She looked damp and rosy and he realized she'd taken a shower, a fact he'd missed while he'd been engrossed in the call.

He rose to his feet, his gaze never leaving her. "I'll talk to you later, Greg."

Tossing his phone to the couch, he reached for Mia's wrist and used it to tug her closer, close enough to drop a kiss on her mouth. "Hey," he said.

"Hey," she rubbed one drowsy eye with the back of her free hand.

"Tired?" he asked, hearing the unfamiliar tender note in his voice. He couldn't wish it back as he nuzzled the side of her head and breathed in the sweet scent of her hair. With her in his arms and the smell of her surrounding him, the weight of his huge problem seemed less.

"Mmm." She leaned into him. "We need coffee. I can make some."

He let her go, and watching her move about in that sleepy fashion was so damn endearing that he went back to the couch and took a seat to appreciate the view. A woman's way with kitchen utensils had never affected him before today, but hell, there'd never been a day like today.

There'd never been a woman like Mia.

Vaguely alarmed by the thought, he took the mug she handed him and automatically gulped a swallow, like caffeine might be the medicine he needed. She perched on the chair across from him and sipped at her own coffee, clearly still working on waking up.

After a few minutes, more clear-eyed, she met his gaze and colored, her face turning the slightest of pinks, the blush nearly camouflaging the charming freckles. "Well."

"Well." He grinned, and stretched out his legs to cross them at the ankles. "What's your favorite morning-after strategy?"

"Um…what?" She brought her mug to her mouth.

"Strategy," he repeated. "To rid yourself of a lingering bedmate."

"Uh…"

"Pressing appointment? You never eat breakfast? Or you must leave immediately in order to gather some facts and figures for an important afternoon meeting?"

Her eyebrows drew together. "That last sounds like you. And very practiced, by the way."

"Practical." He relaxed farther into the cushions. "A polite charade for both parties."

"Necessary because…?"

"Don't you long to be alone again after a few hours sharing your sheets?"

Mia glanced away. "Do you?"

"Yes."

"I suppose because you actually do always have some facts and figures waiting to be gathered for an important meeting."

The comment made him eye his phone. He'd avoided text and emails when he'd called Greg first thing, but the Trey Blackthorne he'd been for thirty-four years wouldn't waste any more time. He'd be on that phone again or his laptop, seeing what had come in from the office requiring his attention.

Except he'd been "wasting time" for the previous two days, sightseeing with Mia.

And he wasn't exactly Trey Blackthorne any more, was he?

"Don't mind me, Trey." She made a small "shoo" gesture with her fingertips. "Go along, do what you must."

"Mia…"

She shooed again. "Feel free."

Feel free.

And suddenly he did.

Wow.

He took a moment to register the unfamiliar lightness of being. *Wow.* Then he set down his coffee on the side table, and drawing up his legs, he patted one knee. "Come here."

Her wary look made him smile. "You're not going to bite are you?" she asked.

"I might." He belied the promise with an innocent smile and patted again. "Mia, *mon ange*, come here."

"What?" Her eyebrows shot high. "*Mon ange?*"

"I read it on one of the tombstones. It means 'my angel,' right?" He smiled again. "Sounds about right to me."

Her frown was thunderous. "I hate it when you're charming," she complained, even as she stood and stepped closer.

The woman found a half-promised bite and cemetery talk

charming? Good to know. "I find your pouting mouth irresistible." He drew her into his lap and showed her just how irresistible.

When they came up for air, she blinked, in an obvious kiss daze that he found immensely adorable, and he told her so. "I should probably hate that too," she said, but her tone held no conviction.

"So." He brushed her hair from her face with both hands. "Where are we?"

Her gaze turned wary. "I don't think you're asking for longitude and latitude."

"Are we sticking with the plan?" Because he liked the idea of having one, that much of the Trey Blackthorne he'd been before the secret was revealed apparently genuine.

Mia's suspicious nature was genuine too. "Uh, plan? What plan?"

"Our Paris fling." He tangled his hands in her glorious hair. "I don't remember you objecting to the idea when I mentioned it."

"I was kiss dazed," she said, using his term. "I can't be held responsible for anything I say when you get me in that state."

Trey ignored her objection and nodded instead. "Paris fling it is. With no concerns for the future or thoughts of the past."

Mia sat on one of the pear-colored couches in the building's penthouse, waiting for Trey to shower and change. She'd placed the box of ashes on the table in front of her and she stared at it with fierce determination, using it as a centering point.

It was some sort of meditation clap-trap that a college pal had once tried to teach her before an exam. A method to clear the extraneous from her mind in order to keep her focus on the subject at hand.

Because today was a test of sorts.

To prove to herself that one early morning spent in bed with Trey Blackthorne and his smokin' body, hot kisses, and talented hands hadn't changed her in any way.

Sure, she'd found that faint red mark on one breast and there was the undeniable physical knowledge that she'd been, well, penetrated—was there any other word to describe the sweet pleasure of his welcomed invasion? Even now the memory made her inner muscles clench and the subtle ache there only served to send a flush of heat over her whole body.

You should have joined Trey in the shower. Cooled off—or heated up more, as the case may be—that way.

Mia narrowed her eyes at the return of Nic in her head, thankfully absent since the man had followed her into her bedroom. Go away, she thought. She didn't need the added temptation.

Because he had cocked a brow in Mia's direction when he excused himself for the guest room's en suite. Claire had taken off for Belgium as she'd planned apparently, and no one would have been the wiser if Mia had offered to scrub his back...or asked him to scrub hers.

But she'd already taken her own quick turn under the spray in her tiny bathroom in the basement while he was on a phone call. Though he'd bandied about the term "Paris fling" again, she wasn't committing to such a thing, not at the moment at least.

Not until she knew he wouldn't drag her into those dangerous waters she'd avoided her entire life.

To occupy herself since meditation wasn't cutting it, she

strolled through an open doorway into a room that appeared to be a study. Claire had set some of her work out—pencil sketches and half-finished watercolor paintings that Mia took the time to study one by one.

They were terrible.

"Mia?"

Trey's voice sent her scurrying from the room. The older woman might exhibit a considerable lack of talent, but everyone deserved their secrets. Why—

Crossing into the living room, she nearly tripped over her feet as she caught sight of Trey Blackthorne, his back to her, his gaze directed out one of the many windows.

Trey Blackthorne, framed by Paris.

But it was more than the stupendous view that arrested her. She knew the breadth of those shoulders, the deep valley of his spine, the feel of his back muscles shifting beneath her hands as he thrust into her body. He wore nothing special, jeans and an untucked oxford shirt, but the fact that she had such personal experience with all that was disguised by those commonplace clothes made the tips of her ears burn.

Suddenly, she wanted to fix those memories with something lasting—a symbol of some sort. Art, but not on paper.

So not a second of it could ever be forgotten.

"We should get tattoos," she said, the words bursting from her mouth.

Instantly she wished them back. What was she thinking, she who didn't want to be in any way changed by a couple of orgasms and a man's ability to say "*mon ange*" with a halfway decent French accent?

But before she could recover from the shame of it, he swung around, a look of horror on his face. "God, no," he said, his tone firm.

Now her face burned along with her ears. "I wasn't

suggesting they had to match or anything," she said, sounding sulky, now annoyed and maybe insulted that he rejected the idea with such vehemence. "But, you know, we're here…in Paris."

"I'll get mine and yours for you, if you're so set on the idea," he said.

She stared. Two tattoos? The man didn't have a single one, she knew that, but was offering… "Huh?"

"Nothing should permanently mar that creamy skin of yours."

"Um…" She continued staring, the intent look in his eyes acting like glue on the bottom of her shoes.

He strode forward and his hand reached out to cup her cheek. His thumb coasted over her freckles. "Except these," he whispered, soft and low, then stepped back, presumably without a care in the world and without the knowledge that he'd just rocked hers. Her stomach was left slightly queasy.

That touch, so…almost cherishing.

"Ready to go?" he asked.

Ready to escape her traitorous reaction to a simple stroke, Mia gave herself a mental slap and stepped for the exit. "Follow me. We have a job…another item on Nic's list."

As the elevator lowered them to the ground floor, she didn't look at him. "No concerns for the future," she murmured, adopting his untroubled attitude, "or thoughts about the past."

Their agreed-upon mantra wouldn't change.

There'd be no change in that or in Mia herself.

No change whatsoever, she thought again as they emerged from a Métro stop. A gaggle of tourists gathered around the map posted at the top of the steps and a tour guide was using it to describe in English how the food of peasants outside the original city center had become the country's sought-after cuisine.

Trey gave the group a sharp glance then he turned his head to survey their surroundings. "We've been here already."

"You recognize this from the day we visited the basilica?"

"We're back in Montmartre," he said, frowning, as clearly the inefficiency rankled.

She waved a hand and started off. "We ran out of daylight then," she said, though it was mostly a case of being embarrassed to visit this particular site with a strange man that first day. Of course, it wasn't much easier now, but it was part of the test.

Visiting one of the most romantic locations in Paris was not going to prove a problem, no matter that she could still feel the caress of his thumb on her cheek.

The mark of his mouth on her breast.

That place between her thighs where he'd driven deep, his thick erection parting her wet and swollen flesh, making a place for himself.

"That's just sex," she muttered under her breath, reminding herself. Nothing to do with romance and emotion and the kind of coupling-up that went beyond two bodies doing the horizontal tango. "Just sex."

In Mia's head, Nic might have snorted.

Out loud, Trey asked, "What?"

Dang. The hilly sidewalks teemed with visitors and she hadn't thought he'd hear over the mix of languages rising around them. Time to curb the habit of talking to herself.

"Well," she said, skirting four women with selfie sticks, "I was going to ask what places you visited on your other Paris trips." That sounded innocuous enough. Innocent, unlike the throbbing pulse those sexy memories had triggered.

She thought his answer might have gotten lost in the international babble, but then he said, "That sounds like talk of the past to me."

Her head whipped around and she grimaced. "Whoops. Sorry."

"No, that's okay. I was kidding." He bent to retrieve a tiny stuffed dog that had tumbled out of the hands of a child in a stroller.

The mother thanked him prettily in French and gave him a lingering look of appreciation as he walked away before she winked at Mia.

She took the obvious compliment with a little smile then hurried to catch up with him and his longer legs. "Did you say something?"

"Only that I've never taken time to actually 'visit' any of the places I've been in the last decade or so…not in the sense of the word you're using. I've had business lunches and working dinners in amazing cities in amazing restaurants, on the way to them looking at landmarks through a limo's tinted windows. But I've never…"

She pulled him through a throng of people so that they reached their destination, hand-in-hand. With her free one, she gestured in front of them. "It's the I love you wall," she told him. "*Le mur des je t'aime.*"

Silent, they took it in together—a long rectangular wall composed of dark tiles with words written on them in white. "They all say 'I love you,'" she added. "More than a thousand times in three hundred different languages."

He glanced down at her, his gaze enigmatic, then looked back to the sight.

Her nerves started jumping. Did he…did he think she was

hinting at something—something about the two of them—by bringing him here? How mortifying.

Because she felt nothing—nothing!—even though their hands remained joined. And even though his hold felt warm and firm, she made sure not to cling, keeping her fingers lax and nonthreatening. Non-*presuming*.

For a moment she considered yanking free, but wouldn't that in itself send the wrong message? She wasn't affected by anything that had happened between them. A woman could have an orgasm with a good-looking, skilled lover and not consider herself changed, the world altered, or see it as anything more than, well, her due.

You go, girl! Nic's voice, of course.

A passel of giggling teenagers passed between Mia, Trey, and the wall, pushing them back until their legs hit a park bench and they both sat down, their hands naturally parting.

Mia dropped hers to her jean-covered knee, surreptitiously wiping away the lingering impression of his touch on the denim. It wasn't her fault his skin left some sort of tingling sensation on hers. Though she'd never experienced it before, it probably had something to do with the man being rich. A sexual, Midas kind of touch thing.

She rubbed harder, frowning when his elbow brushed her arm, now lighting that up too. With a wiggle, she put a couple of necessary inches between them.

"What are those red splotches on the wall?" he asked.

Looking up, she noted them, irregular scarlet shapes scattered here and there. She pulled the ashes box from her backpack and set it on her lap, then retrieved her phone and brought it to life to find the information page. "The creator wanted the wall to hold up the most important of human feelings," she read aloud. "Those splashes—they're pieces of a broken heart. They can be gathered together to make a whole one."

"Ah." He sat back on the bench, his gaze still resting on those I love yous written in letters she recognized and squiggles she didn't. Before, she hadn't noticed the red fragments but now she couldn't unsee them. They appeared to pulse, coming alive like warning lights to remind her, once again, of what she'd been avoiding her entire life, since that first time her father had stormed from the house declaring he'd never been happy. In an effort to chase after him, her mother had backed his midlife-crisis sports car through the garage door.

Mia had skipped school the next day because Mom wanted help dumping Dad's things into suitcases and garbage bags.

What a way to play hooky.

They'd eaten cereal for dinner and Mia had never been able to pour a bowl for any reason again.

The teenagers moved on only to be replaced by a parade of others, often couples who wanted photos taken by friends or long-armed selfies of themselves beaming or embracing or kissing with the background of a thousand I love yous. Not one of them seemed deterred or distressed by the presence of those splashes of red.

"Have you ever been in love?" Trey asked.

She considered telling him the question smacked of the past, but why act reluctant to answer? "Nope."

"Me neither." He glanced over, and she could feel his gaze on her profile. "Which means we've both never had our hearts broken."

"Nope," she said again, then sneaked a glance, because she could tell he still studied her. "What?"

"I'm almost sorry for us."

"*What?*" She turned her head all the way to stare at him. "You want to feel...feel shattered inside?"

"Gotta have a high to go with that low, right?" he said slowly. "I've been so wrapped up in business that I never allowed myself to be wrapped up in someone else."

"I like being independent," she said, briskly rubbing at her arms with her hands. She should have worn a coat instead of just the sweater over a long-sleeved T-shirt.

"But it's not quite living life if you do it all alone and without seeking attachment, right? That's an essential human thing, isn't it? It's like going to Paris but never leaving the limo."

She frowned, tried to disregard his words, then frowned again, having never considered her safe-side-of-the-road attitude quite like "never leaving the limo" before.

All this time she'd thought of herself as smart, not... not...cowardly.

Crossing her arms over her chest, she stared straight ahead as yet another love-struck couple went giggly and googly-eyed and she felt a twinge of envy, not unlike that day at the Sacré-Cœur. Then, she'd even hidden from herself how affected she, Ms. Who-Needs-A-Man, had been watching that bridal couple, the pair clearly touched by something special.

But the truth was, she had been enchanted by it all. There. She'd admit it. She'd been enchanted by the sight of two people in love and she'd maybe, just maybe, in her secret heart-of-hearts, for a millisecond or two, wanted that for herself.

But what about her talent for avoiding attachment? What about her determination to eschew risk?

Change, Nic whispered in her head. *Change.*

CHAPTER EIGHT

AT NOON THE NEXT DAY, TREY STARED OUT THE PENTHOUSE windows overlooking Paris, his phone to his ear. His cousin Brock droned on about the McKinney deal and some issue with the IT department. If he noticed Trey's lack of response, he didn't say anything. The business text and emails had by and large dried up ever since he'd talked to his assistant, Jer, the day before. He'd told him a serious family matter was taking up all Trey's time, and surprise, surprise, whatever the other man—now worth double his weight in gold—had passed on made the vast majority of the usual suspects who clamored for his attention back off.

Except Brock, who'd texted last night to insist Trey call at six a.m. Boston time. Yet even he sounded tentative when he cleared his throat. "Uh, Trey?"

"Yeah?"

"Are you making any headway with Aunt Claire? Learning anything?"

"A little," he said, not admitting his mom was off in another country. "Nothing to share at the moment though."

He closed his eyes, fully aware the truth was going to have to come out. But not right now, when he was still becoming accustomed to the idea. Though hadn't he always known there was something different about himself? He'd chalked it up to being the eldest, to being the one expected to carry the company forward, but perhaps Claire and Graham had treated him differently than the others because of the way he was conceived.

Yeah, it was going to come out that he wasn't truly a Blackthorne and that—hell, a new thought struck. Hard.

While he still shared blood with his brothers, there was no genetic commonality between him and the three "cousins" who'd been raised alongside him. Brock and Phillip and Jason were no more related to him than strangers.

A great…something welled inside him. A disconnect, he thought. Or just emptiness. A void where his identity used to take up so much space. Graham Wallace Blackthorne III, the heft of that gone.

"Hell," he muttered.

"Maybe you should come back," Brock said suddenly. "Yes. I definitely think you should come back."

"Why's that?" Trey frowned. "Wasn't it you who insisted I come to Paris in the first place?"

"You sound tired. Not like yourself."

Trey laughed, the sound short and jagged. "And a few hours at my desk will cure all my ills, right? You guys are getting on just fine without me." Their privately owned company, ruled by the iron hand of Graham Wallace II, didn't really require an Executive Vice President of Operations, Trey's title. They all knew it was merely his waiting position until the current CEO decided to retire and step down.

It *had* been his waiting position. Now…

"Paris doesn't seem to suit you," Brock said, then hesitated. "I'm picking up on something in your voice."

Trey felt his mouth curve up, despite everything. "Jenna's putting you in touch with your feelings. Cute."

This time his cous—Brock—laughed. "Don't think you can distract me by insulting my manhood. Or talk of Jenna, either, though I admit I could spend an hour describing all the ways she's perfect for me."

Trey groaned, as he was meant to, at the other man's smug tone. "Okay, I give up then."

"You'll leave Paris?"

At that moment, the penthouse entry door swung open and Mia walked in, having used her key as he'd instructed. He'd thought he might still be involved in the call, but now, looking at her, he only wanted off of it.

"I like Paris," he said absently, his gaze taking in the rippling stream of her chestnut hair and the peach perfection of her skin. Her mouth, a peachy rose, instantly ignited his lust. They'd not slept together since very early the morning before. He'd considered trying to persuade her back into bed last night, but had decided to let her make the next move. He'd been clear enough that he was willing. "I like everything about Paris."

Without more ado, he ended the call with Brock, his gaze never leaving Mia. He didn't know what was going on between them exactly, and the old Trey would have wanted to pin that down, because he was the kind of man who liked things spelled out in black and white. That love wall—*le mur des je t'aime*—popped into his mind, which was somewhat…unsettling.

Mia came closer, her head tilting as she studied his face. "You look a little…I don't know. Bad conversation?"

"No." Though he thought he'd been a little short with

Brock, there at the end. It was getting harder to stave off the full-blown identity crisis hovering over his head. "It's weird talking to those back home when they don't know the whole story…and I'm not ready for that to be divulged just yet."

"You need a break," she said. "You deserve a break."

"I've been away from the office for days." Despite everything, he couldn't staunch the guilt. "I'm accustomed to being there and people are accustomed to seeing me there."

Mia's hands went to her hips. "When did you last take time off just for yourself?"

With a frown, he thought back. "There was this one spring break during college—"

"That had to be eons ago!"

"I'm not *that* old." He narrowed his eyes at her, feeling a little sick to his stomach. "Do I seem that old?"

"You seem like a guy who's been trudging down a familiar, expected path his whole life."

"Does that translate to I'm boring?"

She smiled and came near enough to touch one finger to his chest. "You haven't been boring to me."

He smiled back, then it died as he heard himself confess, "My whole life I've been trying to measure up and prove I can take over the company when the time comes."

A moment of silence passed, as if she was taking that in. Then she declared, "Well, now you get to slay the demon of expectations."

"The demon of expectations?" At her enthusiasm, he smiled again. "How exactly do I do that, o wise woman?"

Tapping her mouth with her finger, she seemed to consider. "What did you dream about being as a kid? A chef? A cowboy? A—"

But he was already shaking his head. "I knew what I was going to be from…well, forever."

"Halloween—"

"Businessman. Every year my mom put together a costume that was a dark suit and tie. I carried a miniature briefcase to collect the candy."

Mia's eyes went wide. "That is so sad," she said. "No one should give treats to children wearing any suit that isn't an imitation of a superhero's."

"Brock had the idea first," Trey remembered, thinking back, "so I reconsidered my farmer overalls and switched."

Mia's eyes brightened with interest. "You once wanted to be a farmer?"

"Because of corn," he said. "One harvest time we went to a farm where the sugar and gold variety of corn we use for our top-shelf whisky grows." It had begun his fascination with the process of making their signature spirit, way before he was legal to drink it.

"I know what we need to do," Mia said, already turning toward the door. "C'mon."

"The list, right? Nic's list?"

"Not today," she told him, marching forward so he had to lengthen his stride to catch up with her. "We're going to focus on you exploring whomever you want to be instead of you getting hung up on the fact you're no longer who you thought."

Trey mulled that over as he let her—again—lead him underground. Was he hung up on the fact that he was no longer by blood the eldest son, the crown prince of the Black-thorne empire? Hell, yes! Who wouldn't be set on their ass to find out they—

Didn't have to step into the role they'd always thought their DNA demanded.

Now you get to slay the demon of expectations.

The one that had been riding his back his entire life.

Seized by the novel thought, from his seat across from Mia in the Métro car he watched her pull on fuzzy gloves. His mind leaped to a new topic. Exactly what was it about her that appealed to him so? Her face—charmingly versus traditionally beautiful. Her body, average sized but on the delicate side, which accentuated his height and strength and, likely, his ego.

But it was her spirit, he decided, her energetic vivacity that enlivened the facts-and-figures, very dry side of his nature. She was, with her artist's eye and her eagerness to rub a fairy's wing, so much he was not. And because of that, frankly, good for him.

When the train came to a rocking halt, he followed her out of car into the station, climbing more steps until they stood on a sidewalk in a definitely non-tourist part of town. Head bent, she studied her phone, while he zipped up the welcome outerwear he'd found in his luggage. His housekeeper had done the majority of his packing for the short trip, and she'd slipped in a down jacket that rolled into a package not much larger than his hand.

He welcomed the layer against the elements, as autumn appeared to have arrived overnight. "Are you going to be warm enough?" he asked Mia, but instead of waiting for a reply, he slung an arm around her. They headed off, snuggled together like a long-familiar couple.

For a man who didn't go in for much—any—PDA, he liked this, enough that he didn't stop himself from dropping a kiss on the side of her hair.

She glanced over, gifted him with a little smile, but didn't say anything as they passed through an outdoor food market, pausing to admire vegetables he couldn't name, seafood that appeared fresh and exotic, and cheeses that begged to be sampled.

They did.

By the time they'd walked the entire long line of booths, they had more cheese to take home, a baguette, and a bagful of croissants. He steering her to the griddle where a man was making fresh crêpes, but she begged him to wait until later.

"Later." He frowned. Though he'd never been a greedy eater, something about Paris…he didn't want to postpone anything that tasted good. So he kissed her, a lingering, tender kiss, and once he'd dazed her again, he got his way and nearly made himself sick by wolfing down another treat, dripping with fruit.

Following that, they walked more slowly up the street to what he discovered was their intended destination—a flea market. That's when he understood the part where *they were going to focus on you exploring whomever you want to be.*

Besides knickknacks and furniture, jewelry and vinyl records, there were several booths featuring what Mia declared to be clothing that was "truly vintage."

He opted not to mention that secondhand place they'd visited before, the one she'd called "vintage" too, as she eagerly worked her way through racks of hanging stuff. "Try it on," she called, and he took what she shoved at him.

"Something died for this," he said, holding up the article between two fingers for inspection. "And then went through a paper shredder."

"It's a fringed vest from the 1960s," she said. "Give it a try."

"I can rule out wanting to be a hippie without that," Trey told her.

At her quelling look, he slid his arms through the holes. "God." There was a long oval mirror nearby and he flinched at his reflection, then thought he must be mad when he let her shove some sort of furred top hat on his head.

"Who was the leader of that band? From San Francisco? LA?" she asked, her gaze sweeping him from head to toe. "He—"

"Must have had a crazy mermaid in his life," Trey finished for her as he quickly removed the offending articles.

With a laugh, she handed him a heavy coat, embellished with gold trim. "Maybe you were destined for the military," she said, but the French uniform, all the military pieces of clothing as a matter of fact, were too narrow in the shoulders for him, even with his own lightweight parka thrown over a stack of tuxedo jackets that wouldn't have fit him when he was twelve.

"Americans," the shopkeeper said with derision and a dismissive wave of his hand. "Everything so big."

Trey leaned to whisper into Mia's ear. "And he says that like it's an insult. Doesn't he understand that's a feature, not a bug?"

For some reason the comment set her off and he followed suit, the both of them laughing like they shared the greatest joke in the universe. She'd found this froth of a hat from some other century that sat perched on her head and had wound a gaudy rhinestone bracelet around each wrist. She might have looked like a child in dress-up clothes, but instead she just looked like Mia, his Mia, decked in Paris splendor and autumn sunshine. A woman, graceful and beautiful and with a lively sense of fun.

Her mouth still smiling, she spun around, as if unable to contain her exuberance. "Nic would have loved this," she said, and picked up a shawl that she flung around her shoulders. "She would have really loved this."

He stood back, enjoying her pleasure, and realized that it was the first time he'd seen her so carefree. Even when she'd laughed and smiled before, there'd been a sense of sadness about her. A heaviness holding her down.

For the moment, at least, it was gone.

It works both ways, Trey thought. *I'm good for Mia too.*

Something he'd never been for any other woman.

CHAPTER NINE

"LET'S DO SOMETHING FOR YOU," TREY SAID, HIS EYES warm, his mouth still curved in a smile.

She glanced over as she returned the 1940s-era evening hat to its stand. "What do you mean?" With a shrug, she slid the shawl from her shoulders and folded it onto a stack of them, then unfastened the heavy rhinestone bracelets.

Trey took them from her hand. "We need these," he said, turning toward the Parisian standing nearby. "*Combien?*" he asked the man, whose friendliness went up a mere half-notch at the prospect of making a sale.

"Are those for Claire?" she asked, as the seller began wrapping them up once money exchanged hands. She wasn't surprised that Trey hadn't haggled, though it likely incurred only more of the Frenchmen's disdain.

"These are for you," he said, passing over the package, wrapped charmingly in a bag fashioned out of a nearly threadbare, but obviously silk, scarf.

"Me?"

He put his arm around her and began leading her away. "You. In place of those tattoos you were hankering for."

"I wasn't *hankering*," she said with a huff. "And I can't accept—"

He kissed her mouth, short and hard, interrupting her protest. "Take the bracelets. To remember me by."

To remember me by.

Right. She was going to have to do that—remember him. Because Trey Blackthorne's future place in her life was as a memory of…of…

God, she hoped it wasn't going to be a memory of disaster.

She hoped she wasn't getting too close to him, not when her guard was likely down because of Nic and because she'd slept with him and because he was handsome and sometimes sweet and funny and because—

"Have you decided what we're doing for you?" he asked.

And because it was possible no man had ever said such a thing to her. *Let's do something for you.*

It was such a…surprise, that she actually went along with the idea and told him where she wanted to go. Then he took her by the hand and let her lead him there.

"I can't believe you haven't visited this place yet," he said, as they passed through the Louvre Museum security.

Even though this was her first time, she'd done her research and had known to skip the main entrance through the I.M. Pei pyramids and go underground via the Métro. They'd bought tickets with their phones, too, but it didn't appear to be crowded this October afternoon.

Before making a definitive move in any direction, she turned to Trey. "What do you want to see? I've read there are over 35,000 unique items and that if you spend thirty seconds in front of each one it will take you six weeks to view them all."

"Six weeks?" His eyebrows shot high. "We don't have that."

"Right." They didn't have another six days together, which shouldn't make her stomach flutter, not unless she was falling for him or something.

She definitely wasn't doing that.

He slung his arm around her shoulders again. "C'mon, mermaid, time's a-wastin'. Pick a direction."

Forced to make a decision and because all of it interested her, Mia decided chronological made sense. So they visited the Mesopotamian Code of Hammurabi and went on to other ancient artifacts—sarcophagi, mummies, and the Great Sphinx of Tanis.

A wrong turn took them to decorative arts and then French paintings and they wandered together without words, surveying canvas after canvas, until Mia's feet tired and she collapsed onto a bench, gaze on Trey as he continued to take in the amazing art on display.

He was easy to watch.

His hands were in his pockets, his down jacket tucked around one wrist. His hair had grown from its strict cut in even the few days they'd been together and he brushed at it every so often with the air of a man swatting an annoying fly.

She smiled, wondering what he'd look like with it even longer, the strands softening his almost austere features. *I'll draw him that way*, she thought, knowing already he'd never agree to forgo his usual visits to a stylist.

Or barber. Trey Blackthorne wouldn't indulge his hair any more than he indulged himself.

He turned, clearly seeking her out, then crossed to take the place beside her.

She glanced up. "Who cuts your hair? A guy named Sid?"

A funny expression moved over his face and he looked away. "Julio retired. Now I go to Brock's guy, Duke."

"Oooh. *Duke.*" She smirked. "Do you get one of those fancy keratin treatments every two weeks before he uses his platinum-bladed shears?"

"Shall we go up a floor?" he asked, ignoring her teasing. "There's Flemish art or maybe it's German."

She had to giggle. "You *do* get a fancy keratin treatment."

"*Sh!*" He glanced around. "It was only the one time. The guy's relentless."

"Nice, though," she reached up to finger a few strands. "Tell me, does that treatment—"

"I'll kiss you again," he threatened.

"In the Louvre?" she asked, hand to her chest, pretending to be shocked. Pretending not to be thrilled by the idea of his lips on hers again.

"Anywhere I want," he said, in a low voice, beginning to bend near.

But Mia's eye caught that of a disapproving guard at the door and she popped to her feet. Museum security didn't appear as easy to bribe here as at the cemetery. Maybe it wasn't true that every French person loved a lover. "We should move along," she said.

They decided to move all the way to the exit, after admitting they'd both hit their limit. "It's a lot to take in," Trey said. "And your feet hurt."

Still, Mia sighed as she took a backward look. "It's so amazing."

"Don't worry." Trey laced their fingers. "You'll be back."

But it wouldn't be like this, she thought, looking at their linked hands. It would never be with Trey again, whose touch sent a ribboning wave of sensation up her arm. There would never be a day like this one, and she didn't want it to end.

"Let's ride the Seine boat shuttle," she said, on impulse. "We don't have to get off, we can just sit and watch the sites of central Paris go by."

It was easy to buy a pass that was good until the boats stopped running for the day, into the early evening. The vessels were long and very stable, with a roof overhead and glass windows that curved for optimum views. They chose a pair of seats near the rear, on the right.

"Stern," Trey corrected her. "These seats are on the starboard side."

She wrinkled her nose at him, remembering how he'd been raised. "We all don't have a family yacht," she said.

"I grew up around all kinds of boats," he said, with a faraway look in his eyes. "We spent our summers on them."

Nodding, she settled into her seat along the window, her shoulder rubbing his, and she wondered if he realized that despite the news of his parentage that he was still thinking in terms of "we" when it came to the Blackthornes. She couldn't imagine that would change, not really, and she could only hope he'd find peace with the new situation.

The truth was, though, she'd likely never know.

Just another reason why falling for the man would be a supremely bad idea. They were short-time…acquaintances.

As if to match the sudden melancholy of her mood, the clouds lowered and it began to rain. She shivered and Trey pulled her close. "That damn goose again," she murmured, excusing herself for not pulling away like a woman who wasn't falling into some sort of dangerous state should.

"Tell me about your last guy," he murmured as drops ran down the glass, copious tears.

Her shudder was entirely genuine. "I think I liked him because he was too busy for me most of the time," she admitted. "Nic thought standing me up stroked his ego. I thought he was pretty but a pretty big jerk, which kept me—"

"In the limo," Trey finished for her.

Safe. She sighed. "Maybe so." Then she glanced up. "Your last…like interest?"

His grin looked rueful. "I was too busy for her most of the time." His arm snuggled her closer. "Does that make me a pretty big jerk too?"

It left him free to cuddle with Mia on a boat on the Seine in Paris, so heck no, she wasn't going to condemn the man. With another sigh, she rested her head on his shoulder and just…breathed.

On a boat on the Seine in Paris. With a warm man who had her pulse at this very nice low-level thrum, the kind that could ratchet to tribal pounding if he put his lips anywhere near hers. On her neck, her cheek, maybe even the top of her head.

Yeah, she was getting more primed for him by the moment.

But the balance didn't tip for the entire couple of hours they cruised up and down the waterway, their bodies close together, their breathing in sync. When the boat operator came around and told them they'd have to get off for good at the next stop, they debarked, hands clasped again. It no longer rained, but the tree branches had lost more of their leaves and dripped steadily onto the sidewalks, a subtle splash of noise as they returned to the apartment building.

There had to be a song for a moment like this, Mia decided. Sung by Edith Piaf, of course, some slow, torchy number that expressed a heart full of yearning. The air smelled fresh and there were others on the street strolling too, Parisians who knew tomorrow morning there would be sunlight and fresh croissants and excellent coffee, but that didn't mean tonight should be rushed.

Tonight, a half-block from their separate beds, a man should turn a woman into his arms and kiss her lavishly, romantically, cinematic-style as if a famous filmmaker might be hiding behind a nearby car or in a doorway, capturing the moment for all time.

That particular moment when the woman dashed caution to a wet sidewalk and—

"Mia?" a voice called her name. "Mia Thomas?"

As if coming out of a dream, she broke the kiss, her head slowly coming around, her body moving away from Trey's. "Eric?" she said, though she could see the older man's face clearly in the streetlight. It just didn't make sense, Nic's uncle Eric here in Paris.

She hurried toward him, aware that Trey kept pace with her.

"What are you doing here?" she asked the older man.

He hugged her, then looked at her companion, forcing her to make introductions before getting her explanation. "This is Nicolette's mother's brother," she told Trey.

"I'm in the city on business," Eric said. "I wasn't sure I'd have time to see you before catching a flight to Munich, but I took a chance." His gaze went to a car at the curb. "I actually have a taxi waiting."

"Can you come in anyway?" she asked.

"I shouldn't." He hesitated, and he glanced at Trey.

"Hey, I'm going to go up, okay?" her handsome companion said, smoothly taking the hint. "Will you be all right? My phone needs charging."

"Of course!" she replied, and hardly blushed at all when he squeezed her shoulder and dropped a kiss on the top of her hair.

Both she and Eric watched him disappear into the apartment building. Then she turned to him. "What is it? What couldn't be handled with a call or text?"

Eric shrugged. "I wanted to see for myself how you're doing. Victor and Anne know you must be having a hard time."

He didn't say anything about the embracing and more he'd just witnessed, but he didn't have to, because she probably still was in a half kiss-daze. "He...Trey...his mother lives in the apartment building. He's been going through the list with me. Visiting the places."

"Has he?" Eric crooked a brow.

Her neck burned. "Yes," she said, shoving her hands in the pockets of her jacket. Her fingers found the package of rhinestone bracelets and she felt guilty all over again. Today it had been the flea market and the Louvre, neither which Nic had mentioned. "I'm making progress."

"I'm not criticizing," Eric said gently. "I'm not sure I even think this idea the three of you cooked up about taking the ashes to Paris was a good one."

Mia set her jaw. "I know it's what Nic would have wanted."

"Okay, okay." He held out both hands, placating her. "I'll say no more."

"Thank you."

His gaze met hers. "You're going to be ready to be in Nice on—"

"Nic's birthday, yes. I won't forget." Mia swallowed. The grace note of her mission was to scatter her best friend's ashes into the Mediterranean Sea in the south of France, a wish she'd expressed dozens and dozens of times. Victor and Anne couldn't do it themselves, because Anne had a paralyzing fear of flying, which had made the undertaking Mia's own. "I won't let anyone down."

Eric winced. "No one for a second thinks you will. But if it becomes too much—"

"I'll do it," Mia said, vehement. "I promised and I will."

"Sweetheart..." Eric started, then sighed. "Okay, I'll let it go. I'm just glad I got a chance to see you and I can tell my sister and Victor we spoke in person."

"And that I'm just days away from fulfilling Nic's wishes," she said.

"And that you're just days away," Eric repeated. He turned toward the cab, then turned back to envelop Mia in a big hug. "You take care of yourself."

She squeezed too. "I will."

Then he let her go and winked. "That man seems nice, Mia—Trey. I'm glad you found yourself a little distraction to make things easier."

"Right." A distraction.

Watching Eric climb into the cab, she thought that over. Trey *was* a distraction. Not a danger. Not a disaster. She wasn't falling for the man, just...just using him as a diversion to make the process of saying goodbye to Nic easier.

A notion that should make her breath come easier too. A spoonful of sugar to go with the medicine.

Funny, how the idea that her heart still remained safely in her possession didn't seem all that sweet.

When Mia knocked, Claire Blackthorne opened the door to the penthouse. The older woman looked chic as always in brown boots, oatmeal-colored slacks, and a matching sweater with a beautiful pattern in greens and blues embroidered in wool on the caps of the shoulders that ran down the sleeves. Mia took a moment to admire the design, knowing from her earlier conversations with the other woman that she'd likely done the handwork herself.

"It's good to see you, Claire," she said, smiling.

Her hug was as warm as her answering smile. "Thank you so much for coming up this morning, Mia. I hope you're hungry."

Stepping inside, she glanced around, not seeing any sign of Trey. Her belly dipped. Had he returned home to Boston without a goodbye? She'd avoided him the day before, despite deeming him a distraction and nothing more, informing him via text she planned to spend the day sketching in the Louvre.

It had seemed smarter to avoid any more magical Paris moments—the place was a notorious romantic destination for a reason and she'd needed the day and the distance from him.

But she'd never considered he might have taken the opportunity to leave her altogether.

Not leave *her*, she reminded herself. But… "Trey?" she heard herself ask.

"In his room, sleeping or working or…" Claire waved a hand. "…most likely avoiding me. I arrived late last night and he poked his head out but didn't seem inclined to talk."

"Oh," Mia said, trying to ignore the warm rush of gladness. "How was your trip to Belgium?"

"It was a smaller group of students this time and even the tourists have dwindled." She led the way into the kitchen and poured Mia a mug of coffee, somehow remembering she liked it with a dollop of cream. "It gave me time to think."

Over the rim of her cup, she sent the older woman an assessing glance. Though beautiful as ever, there was a new…determination about her.

"Did you make some decisions about your future?" Though they hadn't spoken in detail about why she'd left Maine, between the few comments Claire had made and what Trey shared, Mia knew the older woman had come to a personal crossroads before escaping to Paris. "Are you heading home?"

"I thought I'd address a few things in Paris before making that decision." Claire bustled to the refrigerator, a huge, stainless steel counter-depth appliance. She began removing items. "Including checking in with you, Mia. You started working on Nicolette's list, and that's wonderful, but I'm sure it's brought you some bad moments. How are you feeling?"

Mia found she couldn't speak around the sudden lump in her throat.

As if sensing her disquiet, Claire glanced over her shoulder, and her expression softened. "Oh, sweetheart," she said, shutting the refrigerator door. "You're not okay, are you?"

In a rush, she crossed the kitchen floor to take Mia in her arms. There was nothing to it but to burrow into the embrace and take the warm comfort offered as tears flowed down her face. "You'll be all right," the older woman said, stroking her hair. "Everything will be all right."

It took a few embarrassing moments for Mia to get control of herself. Then she backed away, wiping her face with her hands. "I'm sorry," she said, sniffling. "I don't know what's got into me."

Claire took her hand. "What's got into you are normal human emotions. Grief and stress. You've been under a lot of pressure."

"I don't know about that," Mia countered with a watery laugh. "I didn't do anything for the first month except drink coffee at the corner café, talk to you, and pretend I didn't have a promise to fulfill."

"But you're fulfilling it now, aren't you? It just took time to prepare yourself."

And it took a man. Specifically Trey, who'd traveled beside her, lending a hand, a laugh, and even a bribe when necessary.

"Be kind to yourself, Mia," Claire advised. "If I had daughters, I'd have told them that every day as they grew up. We women judge ourselves much harsher than we'd ever judge anyone else."

"If you had daughters, they'd be so lucky," Mia said, blinking to suppress more tears.

"Oh," Claire squeezed her hand and leaned in to kiss her cheek. "You're sweet."

"No," Mia said. "I have a parent who has only bitterness to offer, and no wisdom whatsoever. When I told my mom why I was traveling to Paris, she didn't understand why I'd bother. She said Nic was dead and gone."

Claire winced. "But not to you. Never to you, not really. Though she'll always be in your heart, you need a starting point for your goodbye. That's here. With the list."

"See?" Mia tried smiling. "Wise."

The older woman waved her hand again, a self-deprecating gesture this time, and moved back to the countertop between the refrigerator and the stainless-hooded range. "Well, let's hope after sixty years I've learned a few things… and I'm about to demonstrate a lesson I've known for about thirty of them."

Bemused, Mia watched the older woman draw a cast-iron skillet from one cupboard and then a waffle iron from another. Though she offered to help, Claire said company was the only aid she needed as she went about cooking a very American breakfast—scrambled eggs, bacon, and waffles.

"Maine maple syrup," she said, withdrawing a bottle from

the pantry. "My coup de grace." With a flourish, she uncapped the small bottle, then wafted it around the room as if perfuming the air.

"What's this?" Mia asked, laughing.

Claire's eyes crinkled with glee and she flashed her a conspiratorial smile. "Wait for it," she said, placing the syrup on the table set for three and then removing the platters of food that she'd slid into the kitchen's warming drawer. "Sixty seconds, tops."

Fifty-five later, Trey Blackthorne stalked into the room.

Mia pressed her lips together to prevent her laugh. He looked grumpy and gorgeous, his hair rumpled and his T-shirt and jeans wrinkled. His feet were covered in wool socks and he slammed his arms over his wide chest, glaring at the table laden with temptation.

"What's going on?" he demanded.

"Breakfast," Claire said without a twitch. "But if you're not hungry…"

Muttering something, he was already pulling out two chairs, then looked between the women. "Aren't the pair of you going to sit down?"

They both immediately took their places and he followed suit, pausing only to pour himself some coffee and topping off their mugs.

"Thank you, honey," Claire said. As he returned the carafe to the counter, she whispered to Mia. "His favorite foods. When his lacrosse team lost a game or there was a minus next to his A on a test, a meal like this would lure him from his room and improve his mood."

"I heard that." Trey dropped into his chair and reached for a slice of bacon, biting into it with relish. "Where did you get actual American bacon?"

"And maple syrup from our beloved Maine," Claire said,

nudging the bottle closer to him. "I've been here all summer. I have my sources."

"I've been here only a few days and I miss bacon more than I can say." He began piling food onto his plate.

"Even with crêpes as your new favorite go-to?" Mia asked.

He looked at her and they shared a moment, both of them remembering the many stops they'd made all over the city for the treats he found irresistible. "That place in the 5th arrondissement," he murmured. "How aren't there lines around the block?"

Claire cleared her throat. "It sounds as if you two have had some adventures," she said, "at least of the culinary sort."

Their gazes broke. Mia took the platter of eggs Trey passed. He applied himself to pouring syrup onto his waffle.

They ate their meal with little further interruption. When Claire made a move to clear the table, her son put his hand on her arm. "I'll do it. Stay right where you are, Mom."

She pulled in a breath. "I like hearing you say that word, Trey."

"I…" He closed his eyes, then sat back in his own chair. "Should we talk?"

"I'm not running away anymore," she said. "From anything. No more avoidance. I decided that two days ago."

"Mom—"

"I'm prepared for questions, comments, rants, even more silence. Whatever you need. Whenever you need it. But I want you to be assured I'll always be here to talk. That's why I lured you out with bacon and maple syrup. To make sure you know that."

A long stretch of silence passed. Mia's heart squeezed as the older woman just looked at her son, her spine straightening. "You have something to say, I can see it. Go ahead, honey, I can take it."

Trey ran both hands through his hair and sighed. "I've spent the last twenty-four hours doing some research and some thinking. I can't pretend I'm okay and that the truth's irrelevant. But I acknowledge that secrecy was advised during that time and that following what the experts told you wasn't an unnatural decision."

"It was a terrible decision," Claire murmured. "I see that now."

"Now being the operative word." Trey sighed again. "I'm thirty-four and I'm old enough to know that what we see today as the right way to handle situations such as this, what seems to make the most sense now, wasn't considered the right way then."

Claire blinked at the obvious moisture in her eyes. She reached a hand toward her son. "If I could only communicate how very much we wanted you. Please believe me."

He clasped her fingers in his. "I do believe you, Mom. But I still have this…big hole in me, though. I'm not sure what I'll fill it with. I was Graham Wallace Blackthorne the Third and I'm not anymore."

Mia saw the older woman was gamely trying to hold onto her composure. "You're our Trey," she whispered. "You'll always be our Trey."

"I'm yours, Mom," he said, nodding. "I know that."

"Okay." She sucked in a breath. "That's good. But you have to know I'm so sorry we hurt you this way."

He nodded, then let go of her hand to stand. "Speaking of apologies," he said, the plates clattering as he gathered them up. "I have something to say about last May," he said. "About the party on your birthday."

Claire grimaced. "I shouldn't have mentioned a secret that

night. I was angry at your father and it came tumbling out. It wasn't the time or place or even the real reason I was angry."

Trey nodded again. "You were angry because we turned your celebratory evening into an opportunity to work. We invited the McKinneys and their presence and talk of the buy-out had no business in that place. I'm sorry for my part in that."

She made another face. "But I shouldn't have stomped out like a thirteen-year-old running away from home. Not my most dignified moment. Though I felt like I'd been on hold forever, anticipating when all the deals would be finally done and Graham would hand over the reins of Blackthorne so I could have my time—or, really, our time together. Your father's and mine. It seemed to get further away rather than closer."

Her son set the plates beside the sink then turned to face his mother again. "You'll have to settle this with him."

"I know. We can't go on like this forever." She sighed.

Trey sent her a sympathetic look. "Does that mean you're going back soon, Mom?"

"Soon? I'm not sure. I know your father's unhappy that I've been gone this long and that I haven't been willing to talk to him about us, but I think it's good for him to know what it is to wait on a spouse."

"He's been surly," Trey acknowledged. "But still proud and stubborn as ever."

His mother nodded, as if accepting that truth. "I'm not surprised. And I'm still going to have to figure out my next step in life. I wanted to follow my passion, but when I was in Ghent I also realized I'm nowhere close to uncovering a latent talent that means I'll become another Mary Delany or Grandma Moses. As much as I love the idea of being an artist, the truth is, I'm not really much of one."

Trey glanced over at Mia. "I'm sure you—"

"Let's go into the study," Claire said, getting to her feet. "I'll show you. I'll show you both. It's why I invited Mia this morning."

Reluctantly she followed the mother-son pair out of the kitchen. Already she felt she'd intruded on a private matter. Again. "I don't feel qualified to pass judgement—"

"*I'm* passing judgement," Claire said. "I'm only looking for support for my position."

In the study, she'd laid out and propped up dozens more of her sketches and watercolor paintings. "Take a look," Claire invited with a gesture. "Tell me what you think."

Feeling backed into a corner, Mia tried again. "Claire—"

"I'm asking you, woman-to-woman, friend-to-friend, what you really think."

No wiggling out of it then, Mia decided. Shoving her hands in the pockets of her jeans, she ran her gaze over the pieces, taking her time. She'd glimpsed Claire's art before and her earlier opinion wasn't changed now. But Mia's thoughts on the subject were no reason for the older woman to decide against continuing.

"I know why you're thinking of giving up," she finally said. "But I don't agree. If you find pleasure, enjoyment—"

"I've found no pleasure in failing to get better after all these weeks," she said, her voice heated with passion. "I despise that I'm unable to come even close to the vision in my head. It's not enjoyable, it's frustrating and upsetting."

"Okay." Mia backed off, then had another thought. "Though you have a vision, you say?"

"I do." With both hands, she gestured to the scattered pieces of paper. "But none of them are...are *that*!"

Her arms dropped to her sides, and the movement drew Mia's gaze to the colorful embellishment on her sweater sleeves. "That's your work, isn't it?" she asked, pointing to the swirls of color and texture created by a variety of stitches and colored thread.

Claire glanced down. "Work? It's a mere hobby. I learned from my grandmother on a sampler when I was nine years old. Since then I've decorated everything from pillow cases and table runners to Christmas tree skirts and—"

"Christmas stockings," Trey put in. "We each have our own personalized stockings—Dev has sailboats on his, Ross race cars—that she made for us when we were kids. They're not childish though…" He shrugged. "They are…I don't know, elegant. We treasure them. I heard Isabelle Caine refer to them as heirloom quality."

Claire looked to her son, smiling. "Why thanks, honey."

"You choose the colors of thread you use as well as the stitches on your projects?" Mia asked.

"Yes." The older woman nodded. "But I get the designs from many places…sometimes I even begin with coloring books. They're not my own."

"But you make them your own." Mia drew closer to study the intricate decoration on Claire's sweater and ran her finger over one whirl comprised of a tight chain of stitches. "This pursuit has historically been considered a craft, a so-called 'domestic' art because it was mainly an activity for women, but that's changed."

Claire glanced down at her sleeves again. "I never thought much about it."

Mia continued to examine the beautiful pattern, a testament to the older woman's patience, talent, and practice. "You know, Claire, women have long expressed themselves in this medium when they didn't have a voice in other aspects of life."

The older woman's expression turned thoughtful, and she

held out her arm, seeming to look at her design with a new eye.

"Claire." The woman looked over. "In my not-so-humble opinion," Mia continued," you *are* an artist, the proof being right here, in what you're wearing. There's places to take this interest and talent of yours and to expand on it if you so choose. I can give you names and ideas. Off the top of my head, you might want to check out the designs decorating the clothes in the fantasy TV series *Game of Thrones*."

"I watched that." She smiled a little. "I closed my eyes on the most gruesome parts, but Logan's a fan and insisted I would like the drama and the characters."

"You should study the embroidery on the costumes. I guarantee you'll consider that art of the highest order."

"All right." The older woman appeared intrigued. "I'll take a look."

"And if you want to better capture your vision on paper or textiles, over time you *will* improve. There are drawing techniques that can be learned in a classroom or even online. You know that. You don't have to be in Europe, if that's too far from home."

"Maybe I just wanted a summer in Paris," Claire said, with a small smile.

"You deserved that, Mom," Trey put in, "and anything else your heart desires."

Mia glanced over at him, glad for both son and mother they'd seemed to have a found a clear path through this thorny patch and were relaxed in each other's company.

"But can I say one thing?" he asked now.

"Of course," Claire answered. "I already told you, you can say anything to me."

"I think you're an artist too, Mom. I remember the Halloween costumes you made, the creative way you wrap presents, the blanket forts you set up on rainy days that kept seven growing boys occupied."

"You were too old for those forts by the time your cousins came to live with us."

"They kept the younger ones out of my room, though," he said with a grin. "I appreciated that."

They both laughed.

Then Trey sobered. "If you ask me, there's art in making a family, Mom. And for that, you would win every prize in the world. That talent is beyond price."

Claire's jaw dropped. Then tears sprang to her eyes and she moved into her eldest son's arms. "I think that's the nicest thing anyone has ever told me," she said, her voice breaking.

Mia thought she might break too. She looked away, unable to look at the pair any longer. *There's art in making a family.*

Something she'd never had, something she'd only borrowed from Nic.

She'd never known a man who had such an understanding, either. *There's art in making a family.*

"Hey, Mom," he said now, humor in his voice, "if you get tears all over my shirt can I talk you into doing my laundry?"

And then it happened.

The worst thing.

Mia's stomach dropped to her toes and her chest tightened or maybe her heart expanded. It didn't matter because either way nothing was in the right place and there was no room in her body for air. Only dismay.

I've fallen in love with him, she thought, doom lowering over her. She'd fallen in love with Trey Blackthorne.

It's about time you admitted the truth, Nic's voice said in her head. *Now I double-dog dare you to do something about it.*

CHAPTER TEN

TREY STOOD TO THE SIDE IN THE PENTHOUSE STUDY AS THE two women researched textile arts exhibits in European venues. Mia's head was bent over her phone. "The Victoria and Albert Museum has collected over 700 samplers dating back to the fourteenth century."

His mom leaned close to peer over the younger woman's shoulder, her eyes alight and her mouth turned up, an expression so familiar he felt transported back in time for a moment, as if he was in the US and his mom was in the throes of enthusiasm for some project or another. But then he glanced out the window, saw Paris, and then looked again at beautiful Mia, who seemed to have almost single-handedly given his mother a renewed confidence and purpose.

Would his mom abandon her paints for an exclusive with needles and thread? He didn't know, but he liked the current sense of camaraderie between the two women as they discussed combining embroidery and quilting and where to find vintage fabrics and antique stitching primers. It appeared Claire had rediscovered her old verve and though she'd run away from King Harbor, he could see her now stalking back into the place and making some long-delayed demands.

Good for Mom. As for him…

Still feeling untethered.

Back at the Vault at the end of September, he'd once again take on the role of "family fixer" and traveled to Paris to confront Claire. Well, mission accomplished.

Sure, so far he hadn't put her on a plane and he wasn't sure if he wanted to, but he'd uncovered the secret and worked his way through it with her. This morning's conversation had been a huge relief for his mom, he could tell—and he was glad of it.

But it didn't leave him in a much better place. While he had a clearer understanding of Claire and Graham's choices and decisions, that didn't change the fact that his Blackthorne roots had been yanked from the soil of his soul.

It hurt.

It saddened him.

It made him damn lonely and he didn't like it.

On impulse, he headed to the guest bedroom while pulling out his phone to call Devlin, the brother closest to him in age. It was only as it started ringing that he realized noon in Paris meant it was an early six a.m. in King Harbor.

Whoops.

"Trey." The clipped note in his brother's voice communicated worry. "Is something wrong? Is Mom all right?"

"Yeah, yeah," Trey said, forking his hand through his hair. "I didn't think about the time when I called. Were you asleep?"

His brother let out a gusty sigh. "No. As a matter of fact I had to come in to the boatworks early to see a guy interested in a seventy-foot luxury yacht. He was on his way to Logan Airport to catch an early flight for Dubai."

Trey could picture his brother, in ragged jeans and a T-shirt, maybe a button-down thrown over in concession to meeting a potential client. "A brand-new build?"

"Yeah." Devlin sounded pleased. "I think he'll choose us."

"I can let you go—"

"No need. He left ten minutes ago and I decided to stay and catch up on paperwork. What's up?"

"Uh…" Another thing Trey hadn't considered. Neither usually called the other just for the hell of it. They'd text over the poor performances of their favorite sports teams or Devlin would report in about Nana's latest escapade. She often drank unsuspecting customers under the table at the Vault, though everyone—falsely—suspected the bartenders there watered down her whisky. "Not too much."

Where the hell had that come from—*not too much*? What was up was Trey's very identity, but he couldn't bring himself to make the admission and explanation via a phone call. The information would blindside his brother as it had blindsided him.

"Trey?" Devlin's voice held that worried note again. "You don't sound like yourself."

How Devlin decided that when Trey had literally said less than three dozen words, he didn't know, but he remembered his cousin Brock making the same comment. "I'm not getting much sleep." Truth.

"I suppose you're spending your waking hours in the Paris headquarters," he said. "Does that mean you've had no luck with Mom? She's still not opening up?"

"No, actually, Mom's…better. More upbeat. I don't know if she's ready to book a return to the States, but I'm hopeful."

"Hey, great," Devlin said. "I actually had a couple of texts from her in the last two days, asking how things are going with Hannah."

The woman his brother had fallen for and who had recently relocated to King Harbor. "Mom knew Hannah, right?"

"As a girl before her parents split. She heartily approves and was glad to hear we're moving in together."

That was news to Trey. Though he was aware Hannah had bought a cottage near the Blackthorne estate and was fixing it up. "You're making a real commitment then."

"As real as it gets," Devlin said, then hesitated. "Mom knows and soon everyone else will too—I'm going to ask her to marry me."

"Congratulations." After seeing the two together he wasn't surprised, though Devlin had been keeping it light and easy when it came to romance after experiencing a painful loss a number of years before. "You make her happy now."

"I intend to," Devlin said, "because she makes me that way too. I was damn close to avoiding love altogether by burying myself in work. Bad idea, bro, just sayin'."

He was saying he didn't want Trey to make that mistake. Crossing to the window, he looked out, thinking of the conversation he'd had with Mia at *le mur des je t'aime* —that falling in love was essential to being human. But now he supposed he never would, because how could he, when only half of him was a known quantity? How could he reveal himself to any woman when he didn't know who the hell he was?

"When are you coming home, Trey? Because—" His brother's voice abruptly cut off.

"Because what?" Trey prompted, frowning. "Devlin?"

A new voice came through the phone. "You haven't been answering my calls or responding to texts." Graham.

At the sound of the man he'd always considered his father, grief stabbed. The wound immediately filled with hot anger, followed by another knife of grief. Trying to get a grip on his emotions, Trey squeezed the device and when he thought he could speak with some calm, he managed an ordinary question. "What are you doing at the boatworks at this time in the morning?"

"I'm not getting much sleep," he said gruffly, echoing Trey's own words.

"And you're in King Harbor?" Astonishing in itself, as midweek his father was invariably mastering the universe from behind his desk in Boston.

"Your grandmother complained of shortness of breath," he said. "I thought I better check in since your mother wasn't here to do it."

"Is Nana okay?" Trey felt a clutch of concern. Though eighty-six, she never seemed to slow down. "Did you take her to the doctor?"

"She's fine," Graham said. "And my visit gave her the opportunity to lambaste me over this situation with Claire."

"I'm glad Nana's all right."

In the ensuing silence, he could almost feel his dad's inner struggle not to ask after Trey's mother. Finally, the older man broke. "Is Claire…is… How is everything there?"

Trey pulled in a long breath. As much as he'd been reluctant to discuss the matter of his parentage over the phone with his brother, he couldn't pretend not to know the truth when speaking to Graham. "You should know that Mom and I talked. She told me the whole story."

A long silence stretched over the phone. "The whole story." It was as if that single moment of quiet had aged the Blackthorne CEO. The three words sounded strained and hoarse.

"Yes. I know the secret." Trey steeled his spine. "I know about the insemination."

"Give me a minute," the older man said.

Through the phone, Trey heard a door close and he imagined Graham had separated himself from Devlin.

Then the older man cleared his throat and spoke again. "You say you know about the insemination." A neutral tone. Cautious.

Did he imagine Trey's mother hadn't shared that a stranger had contributed half of Trey's DNA? Could he think that she'd kept silent about that particular piece in order to preserve her husband's pride?

There was no doubt that Graham Blackthorne had a surfeit of the stuff.

"I know about the insemination, and that it wasn't your sperm," Trey confirmed. "And that I'm not actually—"

"We went to the very best clinic available," the older man interrupted. "I want you to know it was very well thought of, and still is, as a matter of fact."

"I'm sure—"

"They were experts, the very best. The very best of everything. I didn't want anything less for your mother and…and for you."

Yeah, a Blackthorne wouldn't settle when it came to creating someone he'd call "Son."

"We paid for exclusivity, you know," Graham continued. "Anonymity was a given, but after, um, the procedure they didn't ever again use that…that product."

Product.

Leave it to the man to make it sound—make *Trey* sound —like a manufactured good. "Sure, yeah," he murmured. "One time, then they broke the mold. Half the mold, anyway."

"Right," Graham replied, ignoring any acerbity he might have detected in Trey's voice. "And did your mother tell you the clinic sends us annual health updates? We'd get news immediately if anything of concern popped up, of course."

Trey pushed two fingers against the ache beginning to pulse in the middle of his forehead. "Good to know."

"There was a full health screening at the time of donation too. Even a color vision test."

"Great. Even a color vision test." All the facts, Trey thought, none of the feelings. It stood to reason that Graham had gone into the process disappointed he couldn't father his own child and then come out—what? Sure he'd been grinning in the delivery room according to the family photos, but how about as the years rolled on, when he had other, true sons?

Three of them.

Each one a Blackthorne through-and-through. By blood.

The older man cleared his throat. "Trey?"

"Yeah?"

"I'm not good at expressing, at explaining…" After a long moment, he sighed. "The clinic told us that keeping the details private between your mom and I was best. It seemed so to me at the time."

"And later? Mom said she's wanted to tell me for years and that you would never agree."

"I thought secrecy protected us all."

Anger rose from Trey's belly, and he tried holding it in his chest, and then tried containing it in his throat, but finally he lost the battle. "Protected *you*, you mean. Protected you from the world finding out that successful and powerful Graham Blackthorne couldn't father a child."

"That's not exactly right. Not entirely. Don't you see—"

"I see that not only were you ashamed of your infertili-ty…" The back of Trey's neck burned and all his muscles had tensed to the point of pain. "But you were also ashamed of me."

"*Ashamed?* No—"

"You didn't want people finding out that the result of some *procedure*, that the creation of some donor *product* had been given the keys to your kingdom—someone not truly your son."

"Trey." It was nearly a whisper.

"The Blackthorne pride couldn't take that." Trey's tongue clacked against the top of his dry mouth and his head pounded even harder. He thought of all the years he'd tried to prove to Graham and the whole world that he could handle the company. That he could be trusted to carry on everything the family stood for. "*Your* pride couldn't take that."

A tense silence descended. "Trey." The older man's voice sounded hoarse. "Trey, no. Let me…I can't say…" The words tapered off.

More silence. Trey squeezed shut his eyes. "Then don't bother trying," he told the older man, suddenly so tired. So damn tired. "I've got to go." Fresh air was suddenly imperative.

"When are you coming home?" Graham asked quickly.

Home. The leaves would be brilliant in Maine, orange and gold, rusty red. Crisp Boston mornings would be perfect for an early run followed by a hot shower and then a take-out bag of coffee and an everything bagel with cream cheese from Marini's, the gourmet market around the corner from his condo.

But could he return to that now?

He'd traveled to Paris with the idea of restoring his mother to the bosom of her family.

The family that Trey didn't feel he had the same place in any longer. If any place whatsoever.

On a long breath, he tried crystallizing his jumbled thoughts and tangled feelings, only to give up, feeling more hellishly lost than before. "I don't know," he said to Graham. "I don't know that I'll be coming back at all."

Mia pushed open the apartment's heavy entry door and took in the Paris street in the autumn afternoon sunlight, the air seeming to sparkle like champagne. She took the long fringed cotton length of fabric she held in one hand and began winding it around her neck.

"Nice scarf."

She jumped, then glanced over to see Trey leaning against the side of the building, his head against the stone, his legs crossed at the ankles. Hands in pockets. A posture that should have spelled relaxed, but didn't.

Walking toward him, she tilted her head. "What did you say?"

"I like the scarf."

Fingering the material splashed with ochre, russet, and the occasional eggplant color, she smiled at him. "Your mother gave it to me." She knotted it at her throat.

He straightened up and turned to her. "It makes you look like a tree nymph or a woodland fairy."

"Really?" She had to smile. "You're always comparing me to otherworldly things."

"Yes."

Puzzled by the single-word answer, she came closer, studying him. Signs of strain and weariness showed around his eyes and mouth. Her heart twisted and it took everything she had not to reach out and touch him—cup his cheek in her palm or tangle their fingers together. Better yet, press her mouth to his.

Expose herself and her new, unwelcome feelings for him.

Not going to happen, she thought, because that way could lead to pain and bitterness.

She shoved her hands in the pockets of her jeans, but couldn't stop herself from questioning him, the tone of her voice soft. "Trey, are you all right?"

"I don't know what I am."

Again the enigmatic answer. She couldn't think what to do or say next and it was he who continued the conversation.

"How did your sketching go yesterday?"

The Louvre, her excuse to avoid him. Though she had spent the day there in fact, and filled page after page of her pad, while other times she'd merely sat and breathed in the surrounding treasures. "I...it was amazing. Wonderful." In her head, Nic had *oohed* and *ahhed*, even though the museum had not been on her list.

"But you're without your sketchpad today," Trey observed.

She nodded. "I'm off to pick up some souvenirs."

On the verge of leaving him there, she cast him another searching look. He really did seem...almost lost. *I don't know what I am.*

"You're welcome to come along," she offered, her emotions—her love for him—taking over. So much for safety for herself, not when it didn't seem as if he should be alone right now. "I'd, um, enjoy the company."

He agreed, causing her insides to warm and another need to touch the man surge. Digging her hands deeper in her pockets, she set off at a stroll, taking in the now-familiar neighborhood and the sights of Paris she'd never forget, from the tiny shop of the flower seller to the crêperie emitting smells that had tempted Trey many times before. Her side-long look told her he didn't even notice.

Hmm.

Her own feet slowed outside the wrought iron fence surrounding the schoolyard attached to a local corner church. Boys and girls in gray skirts or slacks, white shirts, and black sweaters poured out of a doorway, backpacks worn tortoise-style or slung over single shoulders. Smiling a little, Mia watched them chatter and jostle each other, exuberance at being out for the day showing.

"When do you return to your students?" Trey asked.

She started walking again. "I'm on sabbatical until February." What she didn't say was that she'd be working at the Roger Belton Museum in downtown Boston during November, December, and January where she'd be developing day-long lessons using art and reflecting history for grades three through seven, with the museum's collection as the backbone of the instruction. There had been heavy hints they wanted her to develop and then head up an education department too, but she wasn't sure she was ready to leave her classroom for good.

They continued toward the Seine and a tourist-heavy part of the city where she'd be certain to find stalls and shops with every kind of kitschy memento available for the would-be Francophile. At the first, he remained outside while she perused the narrow aisles and crowded racks. This particular place was heavy on aprons and dishcloths and she bought one of each for Nic's mom. Because she'd forgotten to grab a shopping bag of her own on the way out of her apartment, she also bought a simple mesh bag to carry her purchases.

Trey tried to take it from her as she exited.

It caused a little tug-of-war on the sidewalk, which had them both finally glaring at each other. "I don't know," she said, as he wrenched it from her in a final show of strength and tucked it under his arm, "that you can be trusted to protect my purchases from the notorious street thieves."

"Babe," he said. "No thief in their right mind wants the junk you just paid good money for."

She frowned, then elbowed him. "Take that back."

"I'll take this," he said, grabbing her hand and pulling her close to his side. Then he sighed. "Better."

Better. It was so much so, dangerously so, to have his fingers wrapped around hers and the heat of him all along her body. Move away, she told herself, at least a few inches. But they continued down the sidewalk, joined.

Together.

A man and a woman, lovers, walking the streets of Paris.

Magic.

This time when she entered a store he came along, standing behind her as she looked over the shelves of ashtrays, glassware, and ceramic mugs stamped with colorful renditions of the iconic landmarks of Paris. She held up a shot glass with a line drawing of the Arc de Triomphe on the outside and another with a depiction of the Notre Dame before the fire. "Which one do you like?"

"Blackthorne whisky would refuse to be poured into either," he declared, emphatic.

"Well la-de-da." She marched both up to the counter and passed over cash.

"La-de-da?" he repeated as he walked out. Then he burst out laughing. "What do you even mean by la-de-da?"

Her nose tilted into the air. "I think we talked about how snobby you are."

He leaned close, his breath hot against her ear. "I believe the word stuffy was banded about and we both know how I disproved that."

Eek. Goose bumps broke out as she recalled how he'd addressed that stuffy accusation in that sex boutique and again in bed. "Perhaps we shouldn't go there," she said, working on prim.

"Or we should go there again," Trey countered, slinging his arm around her neck and pulling her close. He kissed her hair, her cheek, the side of her mouth.

Her traitorous heart thumped in approval and her body heated, warming and readying. How could the man do this to her?

Because you're in love with him.

Whether it was her own inner voice or Nic's speaking, she didn't know. But God, she was, she was in love with him and wasn't it tempting to imagine riding the wave of that. Ride high, and forget about the safe side, or the limo, or whatever a smart woman would do who knew she had a fast-dwindling amount of time with a man.

Up ahead was an old blanket spread on the grass beside the packed sidewalk. Tchotchkes covered the ragged piece of cloth.

As she headed for it, he groaned. "There must be fifty different versions of the Eiffel Tower on there."

Really, she thought, why were so many men lousy shoppers? Variety gave a person choices. "I grant you it will take some time to decide which ones will be exactly right."

He groaned again.

She ignored him. "Let's see, I need one for Nic's dad and one for me and—"

"They're all tacky in the extreme, Mia." He shook his head. "You've got to admit that."

"That's only because you're seeing them altogether, in a group." It was easy to select the "gold" metal one for Victor —Mr. Arsenau—which would look good on the desk in his home office. For her teacher friend, Janice, she chose a tiny one that she could clip to her chain of work keys.

But for herself...

"What do you think?" she asked Trey. "The clear, lighted one that simply turns on or off, or do you like this one that lights in three parts, red, white, and blue, the colors of the French flag?"

Before he could answer the seller hustled forward. "Mees," he said, rummaging around in the oversized duffel hanging across his chest. "I save thees for a femme spéciale." With a flourish, he drew out a tower replica about one-foot high, the plastic in purple, orange, and neon green. At the flip of a button, lights circled and flashed throughout it, all to the tune of "Disco Inferno."

"It's terrible," Trey pronounced.

At his appalled expression, Mia decided, of course, she must have it...though she purchased the much smaller clear model as well. As they walked off, she held up the one that most offended him, pretending to admire its garish colors. "Very tasteful in the right space."

For a moment there was silence before he let out a snort of laughter. She joined in and then they continued on in companionable good humor, browsing and arguing over the uselessness and tackiness of each of her purchases until by tacit agreement they took the steps down to the river level and found a bench beside the Seine.

There, they watched the pedestrians pass and the boats float along, the warmth of the sun and the murmurs of voices in many languages pouring like a balm over them. She knew he felt it too, because he sprawled on the bench, his expression relaxed.

"You look contented," she said.

He glanced over, his eyebrows rising. "At the moment, I guess I am. This view is hard to beat."

Her shoulder pressed against his and it felt natural and good and all her danger signals seemed to be off at the moment. "It *is* hard to beat."

Trey's eyes closed. "Why didn't you come to Europe earlier?" he asked idly. "If Nicolette was so eager to visit?"

Ah. That question. Why hadn't she and Nic come before her friend's death had made it impossible? She'd asked herself the same thing a hundred times. "Because…" It was so simple really, bitterly simple. And grievously wrong-headed. The reason why so many opportunities were lost in a person's life.

"Mia?" He shifted, turning to her, and pushed her hair off her face with one hand, his palm stroking the strands, caressing them all the way to her shoulder blades. "What is it?"

Staring into his face, she felt struck by the…the presence of him, as she'd been that first time she'd seen him on the sidewalk. Model-handsome, real-man muscled, he exuded a confidence and magnetism that maybe came from a life of privilege but more likely was just a part of him. Trey. The man she'd fallen in love with in Paris.

The edge of his thumb traced one of her eyebrows. "Why did you never visit before?"

Her tongue came out to moisten her lips. "Because I thought we had all the time in the world," she admitted. "I thought we could dream and plan for as long as we wanted and it would always be there. That *she* would always be there."

His hand dropped to her shoulder, squeezed. "Mia," he said quietly, and there was an echo of her aching grief in his voice. He understood. He saw the great mistake she'd made.

"Then we should enjoy your time here now. Enjoy every damn second of it."

With that, he stood, pulling her up with him. "C'mon," he said. "We have Paris to absorb into the marrow of our bones."

And so they did, wandering around the city, sticking close to the Seine, but people-watching and sight-enjoying, and café-sitting whenever they tired. Night descended but they didn't slow and Mia smiled and laughed and not only enjoyed where she was, but she enjoyed being in love.

Thoroughly enjoyed it.

Throwing caution aside, she held his hand and hung onto his arm and didn't suppress the impulses that prompted her to pop onto tiptoe to flash-kiss his jaw or his cheek or the side of his shoulder. He took her PDA and returned it—ushering her into the restaurant with his hand on the small of her back, feeding her bites from his plate, kissing her lavishly, deeply, after they consumed their desserts and walked back into the night.

When she finally slowed down, he guessed she was tired and suggested they head back. It was close enough that she refused to take a cab, wanting to linger in the enchantment for the few blocks to the apartment building. Along the river, couples were entwined, young families walked along, sleepy toddlers draped over their shoulders. A teenage couple appeared in the midst of a fiery argument, but then they started to laugh, shrugged in true Gallic style, and arm-and-arm strolled away, apparently fast friends again.

Life. Love. Paris.

In the foyer of their apartment building, she and Trey shared a long, charged look. And then, to her unsurprised and certain delight, he pinned her to one wall. "I don't want tonight to be over," he said, his body pressing into hers.

"Me neither." She wound her arms around his neck. Why

not? She was in love and for the moment had given herself permission to feel the feels. Life was short and though all this with Trey was destined to end, it would end whether or not right now they went from vertical to horizontal. "Though thank you for the wonderful memories we've already made."

He kissed her tenderly, then lifted his head. "Today, somebody asked me when I'm going back to the States and…I don't want to, Mia. I don't want to be that man who never takes the time to watch the leaves fall or smell the cool water of the river or stuff himself with one last bite of dessert."

She took in his intense eyes and serious expression. "You can go back, but not go back to being that other person," she said. "Can't you?"

His gaze bore into hers for a long moment. "To hell with a Paris fling," he finally said, his hands tightening on her waist. "You have no place to be immediately. I have no place I want to be…other than in your arms. How about a Europe fling instead? We can take some time to travel around, eat, enjoy… make love. What do you say?"

Make love. Oh, she wanted to do that. Almost immediately. A Europe fling was out of the question, though. Not only was her trip to her final destination in Nice the day after tomorrow, but agreeing to an extended yet ultimately finite affair would only allow more time for Trey to burrow deeply into her heart. Getting the man out of that tender place was going to be painful enough.

So no Europe fling. That wasn't going to happen.

Tonight, though…tonight she could have him again.

Or, to be honest, tonight she couldn't refuse him. She rose onto her toes and brought his head down for a kiss. "Let's go to my bed," she said against his mouth, certain she could distract him from any promises. "I want more magic."

CHAPTER ELEVEN

THANK GOD, TREY THOUGHT, AS MIA PULLED HIM THROUGH the door to her basement apartment. He'd been one breath away from begging. The afternoon and evening had been just what she'd said—magic. Paris deserved the acclaim it received and he supposed the only way he'd avoided its influence on previous visits was that he'd been the Trey Blackthorne that hadn't seen any value for the company or his position in walking the streets, breathing in the air, holding the hand of a beautiful mermaid/nymph/fairy.

But of course, if she hadn't been there, then this Trey, the one who laughed and overate and who'd fed her from his own fork, wouldn't have emerged from the drab shell that was the overly prescribed existence of his previous thirty-four years.

Mia turned to him now, her smile coy as she shut the door behind them. "You get comfortable while I shower."

He caught her hand as she began to walk away. "Company?"

"I think you might have seen my shower. We both couldn't stand in it, let alone do anything more creative." Her fingers slipped free.

She scampered off and he grinned at the sassy smile she threw over her shoulder and appreciated the peachy curve of her ass dressed in tight denim. Perhaps he'd bite her there.

His grin widened at the idea and he drifted into her bedroom that smelled of her sweet-spicy perfume and was scattered with personal belongings—more scarves, a handful of charcoal pencils, an open sketchbook lying on the duvet over the bed.

Of course he had to move that. They were going to be using that bed.

Before snapping the cover shut, his eyes happened to fall onto the open page where a naked man was half-drawn. Headless, a torso, then the top of the thighs, the figure's sex not yet detailed. He took another look.

"Hell," he muttered, and tossed the book to the bedside table, then crossed to the mirror hanging over the dresser. Shoving up his sweater and shirt, he studied his reflection. "That's me."

Should he be offended? Flattered? And why had she left off drawing the parts any man would hope might leave the biggest impression? He crossed back to the pad, grabbed it up and studied it again, frowning at the blurry section, where it appeared she'd attempted to capture the likeness of his stuff but then erased her lines.

"I decided I needed another look in order to get that area just right."

Mia stood in the narrow doorway leading to the bathroom, her hair damp around her face and her body covered in a bath sheet from chest to knees.

"You drew me," he said.

"A habit. I draw lots of things. Everything."

Turnabout was fair play, he decided, amused by the idea. "Then I get to draw you back," he said.

Her eyebrows shot high. "You sketch?"

"You'll find out soon enough." He settled onto the mattress, back propped up against the headboard, legs straight, his ankles crossed. With a determined air, he turned to a fresh page and picked up a pencil discarded on the bedside table. Looking to her again, he tilted his head this way and that.

With his free hand, he made a little gesture. "Lose the towel please."

Her face and the skin from her neck to her collarbones turned a delicious pink. "What?"

"Drop the towel."

"But—"

"You drew me naked," he said reasonably.

"Except you weren't here at the time, uh, being naked."

"Mia," he said, pretending to muster patience. "Is it my fault my memory isn't as good as yours?"

She blinked. "You don't recall what I look like with my clothes off?"

Every centimeter of creamy skin, every occasional golden freckle, the exact shade of peachy-pink of her nipples when they were soft and the darker shade when they were hard.

"Remind me," he said with a bland smile.

After another moment, with a little *hmmph*, she wiggled inside the towel and then let it go. Terry cloth fell to her feet, leaving her damp body uncovered for his gaze. For his pleasure.

Gorgeous.

Maybe his jaw dropped a little. He knew his pants shrank by a size or three as he stared at her figure, the full breasts, slender waist, and hips curved-to-perfection. Her toenails were painted a shimmery pink that matched the color of her mouth as she wet it with her tongue.

Oh, God. He'd have to start thinking of winter—snow, icicles, the mud room at the King Harbor estate that Pam O'Reilly, the housekeeper, complained never was adequately heated no matter how many repairmen came to address the problem. At Christmas, you'd freeze your balls off just removing your boots.

"Aren't you going to start drawing?" Mia asked, and it was Coy Mia talking, a smile just shy of a smirk tipping the corners of her tempting lips.

"In a minute," he said, gripping the pencil tighter. As if he could tear his gaze away from that body, with the small indentation of her navel and the light dusting of auburn hair at the juncture of her thighs. So light, that her sex was not hidden from him, but only veiled, making it even more desirable.

His head went dizzy as additional blood rushed to the lower portion of his anatomy.

"In more than one of my classes we had to take turns posing for each other," she said. "So I'm more comfortable with my body than you might think."

What he didn't like to think about was her nudity being revealed to the gaze of any number of other men. Or other women, for that matter.

Okay, this was new, he thought, tamping down a feeling he suspected might be jealousy—or worse, possessiveness. He'd never turned caveman before, but he was learning all kinds of things about himself on this trip.

"Would you prefer I pose like this?" Mia said, turning so that her back lined up with the doorjamb and he had her in glorious profile. As he watched, the temptress arched her spine, bringing her breasts into unforgettable prominence. He swallowed a groan.

"Or how about this?" She made another quarter pivot so her back was presented to him.

"That," he choked out. "Stay like that." His gaze avid, he took his fill of her, from the delicate shoulders to the small of her back, and then to the rise of her spectacular ass.

Definitely going to bite her there.

"Oh, I should pick up my towel," she said in this faux-innocent voice that set a match to his blood, making it burn even hotter. Then she bent at the waist, legs straight, her posterior pointed straight at him, and he was certain he would lose his mind, if not his dignity.

"Mia," he said, raspy and commanding. "Get the hell over here."

Straightening slowly, she glanced at him over her shoulder. Coy again. Oh, she still pretended she didn't know exactly what she was doing to him. "Did you finish your portrait, Trey?"

"Count to five," he said, "then you better rush that naked glory of yours over here or you won't like the consequences."

Her laugh sounded more like a giggle and then she breathily counted out each number. At "three," he finally applied pencil hurriedly to paper, both which he threw aside when she spun to face him. His arms spread wide, he said, "Move it, sexy girl. Don't make me wait."

He hadn't considered the lucky outcome of her running to him. Her bouncing breasts made his lust spike and his arms closed around her as she leaped into them. Instantly he rolled, trapping her beneath his body. His lips dropped onto hers and he kissed her, claiming her mouth, sucking her tongue into his, as one hand wandered to her breast, fondling the soft skin. The other snaked around to cup her round butt and her legs opened wide to cradle him then wrapped about his hips.

A frustrated noise came from low in her throat. "Take off your clothes."

Another swift, hard kiss, then he sat up. As he reached for the hem of his sweater, her gaze moved past him to the sketchbook and she leaned over to swipe it up. Her lips pursed in disapproval when she looked at the image he'd wrought. If you could call it an image—two curving vertical lines that indented toward each other in the middle, topped by two circles on top with dots at their center representing nipples.

"Picasso couldn't have done any better," he said, yanking off his top layer. Then he went for his belt. "Admit it."

She laughed, then lay back on the pillows to watch him remove the rest of his clothes. "I expected better of you, Trey."

"Maybe I just need a little more up-close observation."

And then he did that, observed, up close, with his eyes and his mouth and his tongue. She clutched at his shoulders and his hair as he teased her without mercy, using the stubble of whiskers that the Trey he'd been before Paris would have close-shaved away before going out on a date, let alone going to bed with a woman.

Mia didn't object, she moaned and arched and all-around let him know she was enjoying herself. And then it was he who was groaning while her mouth explored him until he fumbled for the condom he'd thrown on the bedside table.

He rolled it on but when she opened her legs he went down on her instead, reveling in her scent and wetness, thinking this was Paris too, Mia's feminine mystique, the elixir of her arousal making his heart slam against his chest and his shaft so hard he shook as he slid his fingers inside her and imagined they were his erection, claiming the urban mermaid.

Taking her magic as his own. She came apart in his arms and against his mouth and then she urged him over her body. She cried out again when he slowly entered, watching her lovely face soften and her eyes drift close. Then he was done with slow, the heated clasp of her body urging him on, causing him to drive in steady and strong, to make a place for himself in her clasping, welcoming heat.

Making a place for himself that no one could take away.

He touched her clit as his balls tightened, stroking the bundle of nerves until she clutched at him and came, and he followed after. The two of them, wrapped up in Parisian magic.

In the aftermath, with her small warm body curled in Trey's arms, he recalled she hadn't answered him when he'd suggested an extended fling. He hadn't been kidding. And now he decided it was a great idea, maybe his best idea yet, and he could see it would serve as the ideal transitional period between Trey Blackthorne, Executive Vice President of Operations, and Trey Blackthorne, man who didn't know what the hell he was going to do with the rest of his life.

But for a few weeks he could fool around and have fun and scoop up the leftover glitter Mia left strewn behind in the wake of her smiles and her laughter.

Smiles and laughter that *he* brought out in her. He thought he could be a transition for her, too. They could help each other through unusual points in their lives and then they'd move on separately, more clear-headed for sure. Physically sated, what a bonus.

"We can be each other's transition persons," he said and she stirred, her head coming up to look at him, her beautiful eyes—now the dark green of a settled pool—drowsy.

"What?" she said.

"I'll explain later, baby." He pressed a kiss to the top of her head. "You're gonna like it."

Mia couldn't feel her fingertips, not after digging them into the sheet-covered mattress, and her toes were numb too, she'd clenched them so hard as she came. The man responsible sat on the edge of her bed, his phone having buzzed with an incoming text on his way back from the bathroom.

"Mom's invited us to breakfast," Trey said. "Fifteen minutes."

On her stomach, she buried her face in the pillow. "Oh, God, I can't believe you stayed the whole night," she said.

He laughed, then slipped the covers down below her naked behind and palmed the revealed curves. "You're not glad it wasn't a stranger who woke you up an hour ago for another hot round?"

She couldn't stop the shiver rolling down her spine at the memories, at the casual exposure of her bare assets, at the big hand so familiarly molding her flesh. "I can't have breakfast with your mother. She'll know what we've done."

His palm gave her another sweet caress. "She has seven sons. This kind of knowledge is not new to her."

"I'm certain it's not always right in her face." Mia's skin heated everywhere. "I think you gave me a hickey on my neck, Trey."

"Really?" he sounded a combination of interested and amused. "I'm usually more circumspect." His hand slid to her hip and he rolled her over, his gaze going to her throat.

His eyes widened.

Her hands clapped over the spot where he stared. "It's horrible. How could you do something so horrible?"

Instead of apologizing—or better yet, groveling—he leaned down to take her mouth in a tender, thorough kiss making her forget she was mad at him.

"God," he said, lifting his head. "I know I should be ashamed…but I'm not. Didn't they find Neanderthal remains in France? We can blame the caveman influence."

"It wasn't anyone thousands of years old who woke me up by sucking on my neck," she grumbled, rolling toward the other side of the bed.

He laughed again, reaching for her, but she managed to slide away and ran for the bathroom. "You can shower after me."

When she faced him again, damp from the spray, she was protected by her robe and a new attitude. They'd had their fun, their Paris magic, and thanks to circumstances and her common sense, their time together was ending. Practically over. Today she'd say goodbye, and it would hardly hurt at all, not with all the good memories still vivid enough to disguise the pain.

Trey passed with a brief peck to her temple on his way into the bathroom, and a few minutes later they approached the penthouse door. With his key out, Trey hesitated. Mia took the opportunity to inhale a calming, morning-after, facing-the-mother-of-the-lover breath and adjusted the silk scarf wrapped around her throat.

There. Now she felt completely fine. Completely adult.

"You're my first," Trey said.

She turned her head. "*What?*"

"I had to set a good example as the oldest Blackthorne. Always be discreet. Never do anything to get talked about. So you're my first hickey."

She stared at him. "Why are you sharing this?"

He shrugged. "Because I surprised myself by it."

"Well, uh…"

"How many hickeys have you had?" he asked.

Her face burned. "If you must know, before now, at a seventh-grade sleepover we gave them to ourselves on the insides of our arms."

"Really?" he laughed. "Girls are weird. So what's your opinion? Horrible as you said? Juvenile?" His voice lowered. "Or like what I was thinking, seeing my mark on you, sexy as hell?"

The door swinging open prevented her from answering, though her face remained hot and her knees embarrassingly weak as she and Trey followed Claire into the kitchen where again the table was set for three, including a pitcher of orange juice, coffee for all, and platters of fragrant food.

"I hope you're hungry," the older woman said. "I made chive-and-cheese scrambled eggs and I went out for chocolate croissants and those tiny tarts you love Mia."

They dug in, and when the second cups of coffee were poured, Claire said, "There's some news."

"Oh?" Trey asked, his alert gaze going to his mother.

"The Caines will be back in Paris in two days. They said we're welcome to stay, Trey, that there's plenty of room, but I'm thinking it's a good time to change things up."

He straightened in his chair. "Are you going back to the States?" he asked.

"I'm not quite sure." She hesitated. "How about you?"

"I'm not quite sure either." He glanced over at Mia, but she instantly pretended an interest in forking up more eggs. "Maybe I'll do some additional traveling."

The two talked idly of other things while Mia kept her attention on her plate. She knew Trey was still thinking about that Europe fling, that he thought he might be traveling with her, but she had her own itinerary to pursue and her own heart to keep as safe as possible—though she knew it was like closing the barn door after the horse ran off.

Tonight she'd tell him goodbye.

Claire, on the other hand…she didn't need to have that conversation with the older woman. Sooner rather than later, it looked as if she'd be back in the Boston area and Mia knew she put in a lot of volunteer hours at the museum. They'd run into each other there and catch up on their lives.

Claire would tell her all about the news of the seven Blackthorne boys she'd raised. There'd be a nugget or two regarding Trey, certainly. It would have to be enough.

"Mia?"

She blinked, realizing her name must have been called by his mom a couple of times. Shifting in her seat, she addressed the older woman. "Yes?"

"How are you coming on Nicolette's list?"

"Just two more items," she said. "It won't take long to finish."

Under the table, Trey's hand found hers and squeezed. "Today. We'll take care of them together today."

She probably should have declined his escort. But she'd become accustomed to his company—just another reason to hurry up the goodbye—and so later in the morning the two of them rode on the Métro shoulder-to-shoulder, getting off at the nearest stop to the Parc des Buttes Chaumont, which according to her tourist guide was the fifth largest park in the city and opened during the reign of Napoleon III.

The skies had turned sunny and the air warm again, as if Mother Nature wanted to remind Paris about summer, and people were walking and running on the winding paths and sunbathing on the lush grass. They'd picked up a picnic lunch that Trey carried and Mia withdrew a blanket and the hand-made box out of her backpack.

He had bought a bottle of cold white wine too, and on a whim Mia poured a small portion in a third plastic glass and set it beside the ashes. She appreciated that Trey didn't comment on the whimsy, but only asked, "How did you and Nic meet?"

She smiled a little. "Kindergarten. Her mom has a picture of us standing in line waiting to walk into the classroom. Anne is like that. She'd stay to make sure the first day of school started all right. For the next twelve years, she took a similar photo of us."

"You…what? Just clicked over thick white paste and round-tipped scissors?"

Mia laughed. "Pretty much. We were inseparable from the beginning. Nic was taller than me though, so outside of school people often mistook us for sisters. I loved that. I used to practice writing my name using hers—Mia Arsenau instead of Mia Thomas."

He was silent a moment. "So you lost more than a friend, you lost a sister and a family."

"Oh, no," Mia said, shaking her head. "The Arsenaus are still my family. We're bound by the heart, forever. Though it's not shared blood, love for each other runs through our veins."

Trey stilled for a moment, then threw back the rest of his wine. After that, he didn't seem inclined to talk. Few words were exchanged as they finished their meal of cheese, fruit, and thin slices of red-skinned apple.

Then they packed everything away and explored. There was a lake, grotto, and waterfalls, as well as a picturesque temple copied after a famous one from ancient Rome. One of the bridges had been designed by Gustave Eiffel.

"Why's this place on the list?" Trey asked, as they rested

on a bench, the sunshine washing over them, making her feel like a lazy cat.

Mia shrugged. "I don't know the why of most of them. Just something caught her fancy, I suppose. Of the pair of us, she had the imagination."

Trey glanced over. "She'd be glad you followed through."

"That's the plan." She kept her voice light.

He frowned at her. "What's bothering you?"

How did he know her so well in so short a time? "It's just…I almost *didn't* follow through. I had a difficult time getting started."

"Do you know why?"

She shrugged. "I set aside the list and then it just got harder and harder to pick up again. Until…"

He nodded, understanding what she didn't say. "I'm glad I was there for you," he said.

Mia's heart gave a warning *ka-thump*, like a car going over a speed bump. Relying on a man was a move she'd deemed unwise beginning at nine years old.

She stood up, lethargy evaporated. "Let's head back. Places to go, things to do." Goodbyes to be said.

But before that, one more line item on Nic's list to cross off.

They returned to the Seine in that golden hour just before dusk. The section of the river that ran through the central tourist part of the city was crowded as always, but as they approached, the sound of music became unmistakable. At her side, Trey slanted her a glance. "You wanted to keep this particular entry on the list a secret because…"

She hesitated. "How do you feel about dancing?"

He grinned. "Baby. I'm Claire Blackthorne's son. Though some of the other six were given a pass after my experience, at twelve she made me take lessons that included etiquette instruction. It's why I can reasonably promise I won't step on your toes."

"Great." Mia grimaced. "Though I'm not sure I can promise the same."

He laughed and then they made it to the riverbank, where an expanse of cobbled pavement opened in front of them. A small band played salsa music and a crowd of couples danced to the beat with varying degrees of expertise.

"Is this it?" he asked.

"No," Mia said quickly. "No way. I can't move my hips like that."

"I bet I could make you," Trey whispered hotly in her ear.

She ignored the chills racing down her neck and towed him away, to where another kind of music played—1950s stuff—inspiring these couples to gyrate and grind dirty dancing-style.

"I like," Trey said, stopping to pull her in front of him. He crossed his arms over her waist plastering their bodies close.

I like too, Nic said.

Mia practically snorted. "Keep walking," she told Trey. "We're going for tamer yet."

A hundred yards away was yet another group. A portable sound system sat on a bench, the volume set at high, the strains of "Moon River" directing the movements of the dancers. Mia breathed a sigh of relief and turned to Trey. "Will you dance, sir?"

He smiled. "I thought you'd never ask." Then he took her hand and led her to the periphery of the "dance floor" making a place for them among the other participants—who were young, old, and everything in between.

Her breath hitched as he pulled her toward him, his arms strong and sure. "Relax," he said. "I've got you."

She almost responded she was afraid of that, but instead

let him begin leading her confidently about. "Wow." A smile broke over her face as they neatly sidestepped a pair of little girls with more enthusiasm than expertise. "You do know what you're doing," she said, smiling.

"Told you." He glanced down at her, smiling back. Then it died, and his eyebrows drew together.

"What?" she said, releasing his shoulder, so she could brush at her face with her fingertips. "Why are you looking at me like that?"

"No reason," he said quickly, then looked away. But one of his hands cupped the back of her head and drew her closer, so that her nose was pressed against his neck.

Instead of resisting, she found herself breathing him in, taking in the scent of Trey, his warm skin delicious. Without thinking, her tongue slipped out and she tasted him.

A groan rumbled in his chest.

"Sorry," she whispered. Sorry, not sorry, she thought as she savored the flavor of him.

The music continued to play, seguing into another slow tune. She recognized Bing Crosby's voice. The words of the song. "I'll Be Seeing You."

Her heart stopped. The world stopped. They were still dancing but she did it without air and without awareness of anyone else but her Paris lover, of Trey, who held her close enough that she could feel every hard inch of muscle. She pressed close and let him turn her, shutting her eyes and reveling in this moment with him.

A little panic rose in her throat at the very rightness of it, but then she remembered. This was merely being human and she'd decided to be happy about having fallen in love. She could be happy for a little longer, until it was time to walk away. Perhaps the inevitable fallout wouldn't be too bad.

The fall-in had been so easy, after all.

Oh, girlfriend...

Mia closed her ears to Nic's sympathy and just enjoyed the dance, the last ride, letting Trey guide her until the final notes of the song played out in the descending dusk. As one, they turned and left the area, strolling away from the Seine arm-in-arm. She didn't speak, unwilling to burst this romantic, bewitching bubble.

Trey remained silent too, all the way back to the apartment building, where he followed her down the steps to her basement apartment. Outside her door, he halted. "Mia."

She turned to face him, her key in hand, her back against the wooden surface. "Yes?"

He stared at her, shook his head as if confounded, then stared at her some more. "I…"

You better give him a candy to suck on, Nic advised. *Or slap his face. The man's in some sort of state.*

A man like Trey Blackthorne didn't get into any kind of "state."

But the more he just stood there, wordlessly gazing on Mia, the more unsure she began to feel. "Are you all right?"

"Mia," he began hoarsely, then looked away. "Mia," he started again.

She swallowed, her pulse starting to trip and thrum, trip and thrum, uneven and anxious. "Yes?"

"These days we've spent together in Paris," he said, and shoved his hands in his pockets. "That song…"

That song, "I'll Be Seeing You," which spoke of picturing the beloved everywhere—of never being able to escape the memory of him. Her stomach roiled. "I've got to go," she whispered.

He blinked. His hand came out as if to touch her, then returned to his pocket. "Right now?"

"I've got to pack." She gripped the apartment key tighter,

until it bit into her palm. "I'm traveling by train tomorrow morning. On the high-speed train to Nice."

"Nice?" he said slowly. "Nice, France?"

She nodded. "One final request of Nicolette's. She always wanted her ashes scattered there, into the Mediterranean Sea."

"You left that out, when we talked about her requests."

"Well…it's the last thing, the most important thing." One of her shoulders lifted.

"You left out the most important thing."

"Right." She tried for a brisk tone and ignored the implication that she'd held back something from him. Of course, she had! Her heart had been lost without her permission but she was keeping a tight hold of her autonomy.

Independence.

Loneliness.

Whatever. It was time to move on and put thoughts of Trey Blackthorne away. Later, a long time from now, she could take them out and look back upon them with…with fondness or something.

Mia cleared her throat. "But hey, thanks for everything. I…I couldn't have escaped Paris jail without you."

He didn't laugh or even smile. "This is it."

The lump in her throat grew and the ache in her chest made it impossible to breathe and everything hurt, from the crown of her head to the soles of her feet. She wished she could believe she was coming down with the flu Trey had suffered from when he arrived in Paris. But it was her heart that was sick.

"I've got to go. There's packing to do, not to mention I need to wash my hair." An inane excuse, but what did it matter? She'd never see him again.

"So this is your strategy," he murmured, crossing his arms

over his chest. "Shutting me out because of a need to shampoo?"

"It's practical," she said, remembering the words he'd used on their first morning after. "A polite charade for both parties." Her cheeky grin was so wide she thought her face might split in half.

"Mia…"

"In other words, an easy goodbye, Trey. Just the way we like it."

CHAPTER TWELVE

TREY STALKED THE CITY IN THE EARLY HOURS OF THE morning—he'd been at it all night. There were other men about, walking alone, and he imagined each one was grappling with the knowledge they'd fallen in love. Why else wouldn't they be comfortably in a bed, where he should be?

If only he hadn't made one simple error.

That is, falling in love with Mia Thomas, urban mermaid, and realizing that fact to the strains of "I'll Be Seeing You" and only an hour before she gave him the casual brushoff.

I need to wash my hair.

Wash her hair!

An easy goodbye, Trey. Just the way we like it.

His fingers, shoved deep in his jacket pockets, curled into fists and the gentleman coming his way, in a trench coat and carrying a—self-defense?—baguette, gave him a wide berth. Yeah, do that, he thought darkly, because he was looking for any excuse to throw a punch. Even the nearby lamppost looked promising.

Trey Blackthorne, losing his legendary cool.

Another knock to his previously rock-solid identity. Not only didn't he legitimately own the name he'd always considered his, he didn't possess one of the traits he'd always relied upon most.

That of never letting his emotions get the better of him.

Back at *le mur des je t'aime*, he'd told Mia he felt sorry for them because they'd avoided love. Well, that had merely been a frivolous passing thought. Because the truth was, from the time he'd been nineteen or so, he'd been pretty damn smug about never getting bogged down in the sticky tangle of a long-term relationship.

With six younger relatives to watch tripping over themselves in the pursuit of such over the years—or in the convalescence over such—he'd been happy with his string-free romantic existence. Okay, string-free sex.

Engaging in pleasure without obligations meant you didn't have the responsibility to be there for someone else, to do your part to make them happy. Trey Blackthorne, family fixer, had enough responsibilities, thank you.

That had been fine for thirty-four years.

But then Mia came into his life.

Bright butterfly Mia, strong and yet vulnerable. Mia, who intended to travel to Nice alone, where she'd toss those ashes she'd been holding so close. Of course parting with them would be like peeling off her own skin. He hated for her that she was planning to do that by herself.

Up ahead he saw one of the Seine shuttle boats getting readied for the day. A crew member mopped the decks and he heard the deep-throated thrum of engines coming to life. He jogged toward the vessel and when the guy with the mop told him in French—and then English, when he admitted he didn't speak the native language—it was too early to board, Trey pulled out some Euros and after a brief consultation with the captain, he was welcomed to climb on.

He liked the water and its calming influence.

Here he'd be able to think, or better yet, forget.

Taking a seat on one of the long middle benches, he spread his arms across the top, briefly noting the piled tarp in the opposite corner.

But as the boat picked up speed, the mass of waterproof canvas moved. Trey stared as a kid emerged from beneath the folds.

"Hey," the young guy said, shaking his head to settle his messy hair out of his eyes. A backpack with a patch reading University of Iowa emerged next.

Trey's brows rose. "You're a stowaway?"

The kid ginned. "I had twelve hours to see Paris before meeting my tour," he said. "I didn't want to spend it sleeping in a hotel and I don't have the scratch for it anyway so I wandered the streets most of the night and then managed a couple of hours of rest on the boat."

"You're lucky you didn't get caught sneaking on." He thought of his own brush with the "law" in the cemetery and almost smiled.

"I did. But the security dude let me stay in exchange for my college sweatshirt and ball cap."

"Resourceful," Trey murmured. "What do you think of Paris?"

"Love the pancake things."

"Yeah. They're good." The wind picked up and Trey lifted his face into the cool rush of air. "Where's your tour taking you?"

The kid shrugged. "I forget all the cities—my mom booked it as a birthday present. I'm away from my dad and that's good enough for me."

"Hmm," Trey replied, noncommittal.

"My dad doesn't get it, you know?" his new friend said, sounding peeved. "I don't wanna declare a major just yet and I *definitely* don't wanna major in finance."

Trey went for another neutral noise.

Suddenly, the kid tossed his backpack to the ground. "I hate when my dad's pissed at me though. I hate being pissed at my dad."

"Uh…" There was no good response to that either. Should he say everybody's dad gets mad once in a while? Graham had raised his voice on occasion, when a fender was bended or a window was busted, but he'd never been exactly angry at the seven boys running around the house.

Probably because he'd been absent more than present, Trey thought, and it was exactly what his mother wanted to see come to an end.

As for Trey the teenager being mad at his father… The fact was, he'd never acted out, never rebelled, never had a harsh word for his parents. Maybe because he'd always been conscious of his place in the family as the oldest and maybe also because he'd realized how lucky he was to have both his mother and father, given his three younger cousins had been orphaned when Uncle Mark and Aunt Julie died.

The only time he'd had a cutting remark for either Claire or Graham was two days ago, when he'd told the old man that he knew about his conception. Then he'd acted more fourteen than thirty-four.

And in his teenager-y angst he'd lashed out because…

Because he'd been knocked off the pedestal with the inscription at its base that read Graham Wallace Blackthorne III. His ego had been propped up by that name, by his position in the family, by the responsibilities he embraced as the one expected to fix things. Ultimately lead.

"I just wanna choose my own major," the kid said morosely.

Perhaps Trey should grow up a little and see the situation as an opportunity to make choices for himself, on his own terms. To live life his own way, instead of with the Blackthorne expectations weighing so heavy on him.

When the vessel pulled into its first stop to take on its first real passengers of the day, Trey debarked after handing over a few Euros to the kid. "Get some food," he said. "Enjoy the rest of your travels."

Heading back to the apartment, no sun yet peeked over the tall buildings of the deserted neighborhood. The grayish dawn light appeared still pearly as he approached the front entry and saw a dark figure loitering by the door, its back turned.

Hell, maybe he should have stopped for his own self-defense baguette.

Trey slowed, his eyes narrowing until he recognized the set of the man's shoulders and the salt-and-pepper hair. In surprise, his feet sped up. "Dad?"

Except he's not your father. "Graham?" he quickly amended.

The figure turned, stared. The older man half-lifted his arms then quickly shoved his hands in the pockets of his overcoat. "Trey."

"How'd you get here?"

"The company jet."

Ask a stupid question, get an obvious answer, he thought. "Did you come to see Mom?" He'd seemed adamant against it before.

"I talked to her yesterday. I called and she picked up." An unfamiliar, weird expression crossed the CEO's face.

Was the man nervous? That suspicion rattled Trey, because his dad never showed anything less than 100 percent confidence. His gaze lifted toward the penthouse. "Mom's expecting you then. Here."

"Not exactly."

Trey frowned. "What's that mean?"

"We've been married thirty-seven years," Graham continued. "Deaths...births, business reversals, financial successes. Partners in everything, I thought. In sync."

"Not in sync when it comes to priorities," Trey said.

His father smiled a little. "You were always smarter than me."

"I've been just as guilty as you about putting business before—well, anything," he heard himself say.

"Don't do that when you have a wife someday," the older man advised. Then he hesitated. "Can the two of us go somewhere and talk?"

Over Graham's shoulder, Trey could see the worker at the café up the street was setting out the tables and chairs on the sidewalk, his long white apron tied over his black pants. Trey gestured in that direction, and when they reached the corner, he pointed to an outdoor seat for the older man before he took the one opposite. In Trey's experience, if the waiter wasn't quite ready to serve customers, then he'd simply ignore them in a way that was wholly Parisian.

But they must have done something right, because soon enough they had coffees and croissants and they both focused their attention on the flaky pastries until the silence became too uncomfortable to bear.

Trey cracked. "If you and Mom had a call and you're here..."

"Yes?"

"That seems to imply the impasse is over?"

"I hope so. We agreed to meet in Rome. I rented a villa and we're going to spend two weeks alone. Just the two of us talking."

Stunned by the complete reversal, Trey stared. Perhaps he could see the other man finally giving in after these last months and asking his wife to come home, but to step away from the office for *two weeks*? That meant Brock was going to have even more on his plate, but Trey knew his cousin could handle it.

"Mom'll be thrilled," he told his father.

"She gave that impression." Graham looked down at the table. "I honestly thought I was giving her everything, taking care of her in the most important ways, and…it seems I was wrong. I see that now and I'll do whatever it is she needs. No matter what anyone thinks, your mother is the love of my life."

"Everybody knows that," Trey said quietly. "No one believed that photo was anything but trash except strangers and idiots."

"*I'd* be an idiot—your mother would have my balls if she thought there was any truth to those rumors—and she said so. In great detail."

They both laughed. A little uneasily, but they laughed.

Maybe they could forge some kind of new relationship, Trey thought, though his stomach hollowed wondering how that might be.

Clearing his throat, he said, "So—"

"Trey—"

More awkward chuckles until the older man gestured at him. "You go."

"I'm just curious about what happened. Why did you

change your mind and call Mom? And why are you here and not on your way to Italy?" If he'd agreed to meet with Trey's mother in Rome, what was he doing drinking coffee here with him in Paris?

"Because after our phone conversation, I realized I couldn't risk losing your mother." The other man paused. "And I couldn't risk losing you."

"I—"

Graham held up his hand. "The problem with that damn secret and you finding it out this way was that it let you develop a mistaken impression. To be honest, son, I think I'd have been much happier taking the truth to my grave."

Son. "But the truth *is* out."

"Right." Graham inhaled a breath through his nose. "And I've never been so damn scared in my life as when you said...when you said..."

"That you were ashamed of me." Trey had hit the nail on the head with that one, right? "Because I'm not truly your biological son."

A muscle in the older man's jaw ticked. "I've been your parent for more than thirty-four years. Don't you think our relationship has moved well beyond the confines of biology by now, Trey?"

Well, he had a point. "I..."

"When I was a young man in my prime, it was a blow, I won't lie, to think I couldn't father children. We wanted kids, your mother and I, and I pressed for the procedure as early in our marriage as I did because I wanted to make her happy so damn badly. To make *us* happy."

"Okay."

"But now, I'm not ashamed of you or worried about anybody learning of that choice we made."

"Not now that you have three biological sons."

"Damn it, Trey," his father began hotly, then visibly took a minute to cool his temper. "You're not listening."

Maybe he wasn't. His mother had said Graham wasn't good at hearing and he didn't want to be like the other man in that way. He sat back in his chair. "What am I missing?"

"The reason I've been afraid all these years. The reason that I…that I couldn't breathe let alone think when you told me you knew about the donor insemination."

Trey sat forward. "And that reason is…?"

Graham met his gaze. "I never wanted you to feel you weren't a true Blackthorne or truly my son. I never wanted you not to see me as your father. Losing you, Trey—I've been afraid of that for thirty-four years."

Slumping against the back of his chair, Trey stared at the other man. "I…" The words circled in his head, along with his own feelings—betrayal, confusion, and now…relief. His father's fear meant—

"I love you, son," Graham said.

That.

"God," Trey choked out. He put his hand over his eyes. "I don't know what…"

Then he heard Mia's voice, the words she'd spoken in the park. *The Arsenaus are still my family. We're bound by the heart, forever. Though it's not shared blood, love for each other runs through our veins.*

His hand dropped, he looked at his father and realized he was certain of at least something. "I might not know exactly what all this means for us, for me and the rest of the Blackthornes, and where I fit in now, but I do know I love you too, Dad. You and the family are not going to lose that."

His father's gaze didn't leave his face. "Or you?"

Trey breathed in, nodded. "Or me. You're not going to lose me."

"Good." Briefly, the older man closed his eyes, tension leaving his face. "That's good."

Shortly after, they left the café but didn't head for the apartment, opting for a walk along the Seine. "I'm not taking any chances," Graham admitted. "Your mom wants to meet me in Rome and that's where she'll see me first."

Trey couldn't help smiling at his father. "Hedging your bets?"

"Haven't I taught you the value in that?"

"Yeah, Dad," he replied. "You taught me that and heck of a lot of other things."

There was a pause, then Graham looked over. "Does that include letting a good woman get away from you? Because that lesson I'd regret."

His head whipped toward his father. "What?"

Dad shrugged. "Just a guess. Your mom said you seemed quite interested in a young woman staying in the apartment building. I found you wandering around Paris in the early morning hours wearing what looks like yesterday's clothes. Not to mention a long face. Doesn't appear you spent last night with her."

"Both you and Mom are a pair of nosy gossips," Trey said, frowning.

"When it comes to our kids…hell yeah." Graham let a beat pass. "Well, what's going on with you and this Mia?"

Mia…

An ache of—something, God, could it be longing?— coursed through him. He felt weak in the knees and then angry in the wake of it. Damn, he didn't want this for himself. His life was enough of a mess without adding Mia into the mix.

But she made him feel…good. And she made him see a way through the mess. Remember that trip to the flea market? *We're going to focus on you exploring whomever you want to be instead of you getting hung up on the fact you're no longer who you thought.*

"She's leaving," he said shortly, recalling that, too. "Probably already gone. Off to Nice. We had a fling, that's all."

"Did you tell her how you feel?"

Right. Look like a fool when she didn't reciprocate his feelings? He shrugged and shook his head at the same time.

His dad grunted. "Stupidity doesn't just come down through the genes. Good to know."

"What?" He glared at his father.

"I let my wife get away for almost five months because I was too full of pride not to tell her that I needed her and that I'd do anything necessary to make her happy and keep her beside me."

"Dad—"

"She's going to forgive me and take me back because she needs me, too. If you feel like your mother thinks you do about this Mia…I bet you do something for your woman as well."

Trey thought of how he'd made her smile and laugh. How she'd not tackled Nicolette's list until she had him at her side. Maybe she could scatter those ashes alone, but wouldn't it make him feel better knowing she had him to turn to when that last task was completed?

No matter whether she reciprocated his feelings or what the future held for them, if that's what she needed, Trey could hold her and comfort her.

Love her.

Mia had a failing. Well, she had many failings, but right now the failing staring her in the face was that she overpacked. And not only had she brought too many clothes to Paris, she'd bought a few things too, and not just the silly souvenirs. She stared at her luggage open on her narrow basement apartment bed—the commonplace bag on wheels every traveler used, then an emergency duffel that she'd brought from home, and finally an emergency emergency duffel, this one's front printed with a map of the Paris Métro.

All three were so full they couldn't be zipped.

"Good thing I have plenty of space in my bag," a man's voice said.

Her gaze swung to Trey. She couldn't even demand to know how he'd gotten in, because she'd left the front door open, the train station her destination as soon as she found a way to shut her bags. Not to mention haul all three of them up the stairs and out the door. She had a vision of herself, handle of the rolling suitcase in one hand, strap of one overstuffed duffel over a shoulder so it banged on her right hip, the other strap around her other shoulder so it banged on her left hip with every step. Her backpack thumping against her spine.

"I'll return in just a minute," he said. "Don't move."

Our hero, Nic sighed in Mia's head.

If she wasn't so exhausted from a night without sleep, Mia would have protested. But she was beyond tired and then there was the preoccupation she had with today's task distracting her. It was Nic's birthday. They'd spent every one of them together since turning six years old. At sunset, Mia had vowed to scatter the last tangible part of her best friend into the sea, per Nic's wishes.

The heaviness of the responsibility seemed to numb Mia to the world around her, her mind going slow and her body turning heavy. So thank God Trey returned within a few moments to repack her belongings and get them and her to the train station. One visit to the ticket office and he procured adjoining seats for the six-hour journey. She dozed during most of it and when she awoke she pretended to be asleep—and pretended that her head wasn't using Trey's shoulder as a pillow.

If she told him her exact plans, she didn't remember it clearly, but once they left the Nice train station he ushered her toward a waiting car. Even on the short walk to the long vehicle she registered the differences from Paris. Buildings were the colors of sherbet and terra-cotta and the warm temperature proved summer liked lingering in the south of France. The sun seemed to almost bleach the air which smelled like salt and sheets dried on the line.

She took a big gulp of it and felt tears sting the corners of her eyes. "Nic should be here."

Trey helped her into the back seat of the car and in a side panel found a small packet of tissues. He closed her fingers around it. "She is here, baby, she is."

As the car took them in the direction of the sea, Mia recalled more particulars of her plan. "I reserved a room," she said.

"I did, too," Trey replied. "We're going to rent a boat now and while we're out, Henri will check us into the hotel and deliver our bags. They'll be waiting for us in our suite when we're done."

"A boat?" Her brows drew together as she considered this. "I was just going to walk along the beach."

"There's too many people and the wind would likely blow in the wrong direction." Trey grimaced. "You'd end up with ash all over you."

The idea of it tickled her funny bone. She laughed,

thinking of trying to dodge a cloud of ashes like someone intent on avoiding a swarm of bees. "Nic would think that funny," she said.

I do think that's funny.

Trey pushed Mia's hair off her forehead. "Still, we're taking a boat."

Again, her uninvited companion managed all the details. One minute she was riding in a gleaming car with a rich leather interior, the next she was on a dock in the open air, the magnificent Mediterranean Sea, the color a you-had-to-see-it turquoise, extending to the horizon. Trey stood on the deck of a speedboat, his legs spread, rocking easily with the movement of the vessel. He held out his hand to her, his fingers curling in a small gesture of encouragement.

"What are you doing?" she asked, suddenly perplexed. The man looked born to be here, as easy on the French Riviera as another man might be at the ballpark. The breeze ruffled his dark hair, long enough now to become truly disordered. He ignored it though, his gaze hidden behind aviator sunglasses, the tails of his expensive-yet-casual cotton shirt flapping. When he said nothing, she asked again. "What are you doing with *me*?"

Instead of answering, he smiled and leaned up to take her elbow and gently guide her into the boat. They took seats beside each other and his arm circled her waist while the driver settled behind the wheel and then they shot across the water, heading away from shore. There were no other vessels nearby when their boat slowed, then stopped.

It sat in the water, gently rolling from side to side. The air had cooled and she shivered. Trey drew her closer to him, sharing his body heat. "Are you ready, sweetheart?" he asked gently.

Her hands clutched the box. Trey must have taken care of

that too, since she didn't remember withdrawing it from her backpack. Glancing down, she brushed her thumb over the lid. "I'm not sure I can do this. I'm..." She gave up, shrugging.

He hooked his sunglasses in the open collar at his throat and studied her face, his brows drawn together. "Are you seasick? Are you worried about falling into the water because you can't swim?"

"No, I'm not seasick and I know how to swim." She stood up, swayed a little, and Trey stood too, steadying her with a hand at her waist.

"Your best bet is at the stern of the boat," he said. At her raised eyebrow, he gave a little smile. "The back."

With him hovering behind her, she made her way to the rear of the vessel. She stood there, the box in her hand, trying to imagine herself letting its content go.

Letting Nic go.

She glanced over her shoulder at Trey, his gaze trained on her face, his expression full of sympathy. "Why are you here?" she asked again.

His eyebrows rose and he glanced at the box, glanced back at her. "You want to do this now? First?"

She didn't know what he meant. Well, of course she did. It was she who'd demanded to know why he'd gone to all this effort to accompany her when she'd said her goodbye the night before.

Why don't you talk, Mia? Why don't you tell him the truth?

She was supposed to admit to Trey she'd fallen in love with him in just their limited time together? It was such a risk, such an invitation to disaster—

Such a joy for you, little sister.

Mia looked out at the sea, the immensity of it overwhelming. God. The truth was, her feelings were just that big for the man, just that deep. In comparison, they made these fears and doubts as insubstantial as dust. Her hands tightened on the box and she looked down at it again. Hadn't her best friend's passing taught her the most important lesson, more essential than anything her parents' disastrous marriage had etched?

She knew now that life was short and squandering any of its sweetness was the biggest danger, the biggest mistake of all.

Refusing to bend to further qualms, she spun to face Trey Blackthorne, and stood for another moment stunned by his model good looks, the very masculine structure of his form, the smile that grew in his eyes and then tugged up the corners of his lips.

He had great lips.

They moved, making the shape of her name. Then his big hand cupped her cheek. "I'm going first, because I'm not too proud to lay it out there or too stubborn to let your ditching me to wash your hair get under my skin." His white teeth flashed.

"Trey," she whispered, her heart starting to pound.

"I'm in love with you, Mia Thomas. I want to start something with you, something lasting."

She stared, almost knocked overboard, because she'd been ready to propose that fling with him in Paris, Prague, Boston, or Beijing. Even something temporary would have been worth pursuing, just to have more time with this gorgeous man who thought her a mermaid, an angel. But this…

He *loved* her. "I'm in love with you too," she whispered.

"I know," he said, proving his Blackthorne arrogance didn't stay down for long. His expression filled with humor.

"I saw it on your face when I brought down that extra suitcase."

She went to play-smack him and realized she still held Nic's ashes. Her breath caught.

Trey sobered too. "You can do it, sweetheart." He glanced at the sky. "Sunset. Time to grant her last wish."

His hands on her shoulders turned her again toward the sea. Mia held the box in one palm and placed the other over the lid. "She's not really here," she said aloud, suddenly realizing the truth. "No more than she's in dandelion fluff or that wisp of cloud on the horizon."

"Or she's in both of those and everything else too," Trey said, pressing his cheek to hers.

Holding that thought in her head, Mia lifted the lid and leaned out, over the side of the boat, letting the ashes slide free, spilling like sand in a bottle into the blue, blue sea under the orange, pink, and red sky. Nic, returning and arriving, both at once.

Goodbye. Hello.

One big circle as never-ending as love.

Later, Mia sat in Trey's arms on the balcony of their hotel suite, champagne cooling in a bucket at their elbows, watching night descend.

Even in darkness, new life, new love beginning.

Trey's head bent to her ear. "You okay?"

She relaxed more heavily into the cradle of his body. "For two people who'd never been in love, we recognized the symptoms pretty quickly."

"Yeah, especially for two people who never *wanted* to be in love."

Shifting on his lap, she took a better look at his face. "Regrets?" she asked, though she knew the answer.

He laughed and stood, scooping her up to head for the bedroom. "Ask me again when both of us can breathe."

"Promises, promises," she said, laughing and clutching at his shoulders. It felt good to laugh. It felt good to see her man playful and relaxed, his hair falling over his forehead. They were good for each other.

Such joy.

EPILOGUE

TREY GRIPPED MIA'S HAND TIGHTLY, TRYING TO WARM HER cold fingers which trembled slightly in his hold as they approached the front entrance of the house in King Harbor. "Sweetheart," he said, drawing her closer to his side. "It's going to be okay. There's no need to be nervous."

"Right," she said, lifting her chin.

But he could tell his words didn't put her at ease. He supposed the view, impossibly beautiful as it was with the autumn backdrop of gray-green ocean and deeply blue sky didn't help, nor the imposing house in the foreground, with its many bedrooms, multiple terraces, and landscaping lush and well-tended. They'd walked around to the front entrance though he'd left his car in the driveway, near the cavernous garage. No other vehicles had been in evidence, but he knew his parents to be at the estate, already home for a few days after their own sojourn in Rome.

Before entering the house, he leaned down for a quick kiss. "Please don't worry. Think about it. You know Mom. And Nana's a hoot."

"Sure."

Trey had a sudden thought. "But don't let Nana challenge you to a whisky drinking contest," he said quickly. "Promise me."

Mia nodded. "I've never actually tasted whisky."

"Never tasted whisky?" His head spun. How had this never come up? It must have been all that wine they'd been drinking in France, and then in Spain and Portugal where they'd traveled next, chasing the last of the summer. "Good God. Don't tell anybody that."

Now he found his own nerves jangling and he reached into his pocket with his free hand and found Grandpop's horn card case that he continued to carry. Touching the talisman calmed him and he was about to reach for the knob when the door swung open.

"You're here." With her husband at her elbow, Claire beamed widely, and Trey wasn't surprised she hadn't let the housekeeper be the first to greet them. "I'm so glad to see you."

She hugged Mia and then Trey. Graham stepped up next, formally introducing himself and shaking Mia's hand. Then he said, "Oh, you probably think I'm a pompous bore," before he gathered her in for a brief but warm embrace.

When she was on her feet again, Trey's dad turned to him. They smiled at each other. It wasn't clear who moved first, but then they were hugging too, and that one moment seemed to close any lingering separation between them. "Son," his dad said, then clapped him hard enough on his back to bruise.

They stepped away from each other, the smiles now grins.

Yeah. It was going to be okay.

Mia must have thought so too, because she slipped her small hand in his and leaned her cheek against his shoulder. Unspoken support, unspoken happiness.

Both clear as a bell to him.

"This way," Claire said, indicating the shortest route to the great room. It was the usual gathering place when the house was being used just by family. She led to the arched entrance, then stopped and turned, watching their reaction as they stepped inside.

Trey didn't see the immense glass doors that opened to the wide terrace in the summers, the one that offered another spectacular ocean view. He didn't see the scattering of furniture, including the grand piano that Claire had tried to encourage—without success—seven Blackthorne boys to master.

Instead, his gaze took in the six tall men and six beautiful women all on their feet, their gazes trained on him and Mia, every expression expectant. "Surprise," Devlin said, from his place beside his lovely Hannah. "And welcome home."

Trey found he had to clear his throat of the strange lump there. "I thought I might see you this visit, Dev, since you're solidly based in King Harbor, but everybody?"

Even his youngest brother Logan was there, recently relocated to Seattle with his sweetheart, game designer Piper. Why, they must have barely had time to fill up on salmon and Dungeness crab before returning to the land of chowder and lobster rolls. Logan lifted his hand to his forehead and gave a two-fingered salute.

Then his cousin Jason, who lived in LA, came forward to shake his hand and deliver another friendly blow to Trey's shoulder. "Mallory and I couldn't bear to miss meeting the woman who inspired you to take a month away from your desk."

"Right." Trey smiled, then glanced at Brock, standing with a smiling Jenna. Though Trey wouldn't be stupid enough to talk business this afternoon and with this crowd in attendance, he and his youngest cousin had already exchanged some ideas about shifting and adjusting the duties and responsibilities at Blackthorne Enterprises. When his dad stepped down as CEO—and it seemed that would be sooner than later—they both would dually run the business, leaving plenty of time for leisure...or just plain living.

Ross caught his eye. "We had to come too," his cousin said, slinging his arm around his fiancée Holly, who worked at their distillery in Lexington, Kentucky, "though I kept to the speed limit the entire way." The innocent expression he donned made Trey only shake a finger at him.

"Good to have you back." Phillip grinned, and the Blackthorne cousin who'd felt the loss of his folks so deeply appeared completely at ease, with the girl who'd once got away now securely on his arm.

Trey grabbed Mia's wrist and tugged her to the middle of the semicircle. "Everyone, this is Mia Thomas." Lifting her left hand, he kissed the back of it and showed off the engagement ring they'd found at a jeweler's in Lisbon. It was "vintage" or "used" according to your point of view. "Soon to be Mia Blackthorne. We're marrying at Christmas and we hope to tie the knot here."

The crowd went wild at that. He and Mia had already shared the news with the Arsenau family who'd been nearly as noisy with their approval. Trey realized that protocol might suggest they shouldn't beat Devlin and Hannah, Ross and Holly, Phillip and Ashley, and Brock and Jenna to the altar since the other pairs were engaged before them, but he'd told Mia it was the prerogative of being oldest.

As she was deluged by Blackthornes, it was hard to help her with identifying each member of his family through the loud exclamations, handshakes, hugs, and warm welcomes from his brothers, cousins, and their women. Ultimately Trey threw in the towel and backed off, finding Nana uncharacteristically seated at the periphery. Concerned, he crouched in front of her and took her hands. "Are you feeling okay?"

"Oh, I'm just fine," she said, nodding to the short crystal glass of whisky on the small table beside her and then at the large knot of celebrating Blackthornes. "Enjoying the show."

He glanced over his shoulder. "It's a good show."

"For you, my darling," she said. "To prove they're with you always, as you're always one of them."

Another lump grew in his throat. His parents, with his permission, had explained to the family the circumstances of his conception. While Graham and Claire had been in Rome, reconciled quite quickly despite—or maybe because of—those months apart, they'd video-conferenced with the other six of Trey's generation. Since, he'd fielded calls from each and every one, filled with assurances and affection, but seeing them here for him…

"It means everything," he told Nana, realizing that this time the "family fixer" was the one being sorted out. Certainly there would still be moments ahead when he'd wonder about the missing biological half of himself, but there would always be these people, this clan at his back.

His people.

"Blackthornes are nothing if not loyal," Nana said.

Then Graham was shouting them all down, demanding quiet. Trey stood and crossed to Mia as drinks were offered to those without. His woman didn't blink an eye when handed a glass of whisky, poured from a bottle of their premium brand, Blackthorne Gold.

The patriarch held up his own glass, his other hand wrapped around that of his wife. "Since May, we've been in flux, but now we've come out of those unstable times, better and bigger than before. We—and I include myself—have taken our lumps, searched our souls, and discovered essential truths."

A spirited round of applause followed.

Graham paused until there was quiet again. "So here's to us, and finding pride in learning, pride in change, pride in give and take. But one thing has not and will not be altered, and that's pride in family." His voice rose. "To the Blackthornes!"

They all toasted and drank.

Mia managed to smother her small cough at her first taste of whisky and then Trey stepped up, his gaze meeting hers. "I love you," he whispered. He might be Graham Wallace Blackthorne III, but he knew he'd always be first in her eyes, and that meant everything. God, how lucky he was to have her. How glad he was that his crisis of identity had led him to her.

He thought he owed Nicolette Arsenau a little gratitude as well.

Damn straight.

Mia had shared that sometimes she heard her best friend's voice in her head and Trey thought sometimes she spoke in his too. It proved how much he'd changed that the whimsical idea didn't make him blink. Just more magic that his urban mermaid had brought into his life. In return, he would care for her always and do all he could to make her happy.

Now he turned his gaze from his fiancée to sweep it over the rest of the assemblage, from Nana, to his parents, to his brothers and cousins and the women beside them.

"To what remains unbroken and to that common thing running through all our veins," he said, lifting his glass of Blackthorne Gold. "To love."

The End

ABOUT THE AUTHOR

Christie Ridgway is the author of over 60 novels of contemporary romance. All her books are both sexy and emotional and tell about heroes and heroines who learn to believe in the power of love. A *USA Today* bestseller, Christie is a six-time RITA finalist and has won best contemporary romance of the year and career achievement awards from *Romantic Times Book Reviews*.

A native of California, Christie now resides in the southern part of the state with her family. Inspired by the beaches, mountains, and cities that surround her, she writes tales of sunny days and steamy nights. For a complete list of books, excerpts, and news on the latest going on with Christie:

Visit Christie's website
http://christieridgway.com

facebook.com/ChristieRidgway

twitter.com/christieridgway

Made in the USA
Monee, IL
09 May 2022